Once Upon A Dream

by Evelyn Ferguson

Copyright © Evelyn Ferguson

Once Upon A Dream
by Evelyn Ferguson

Printed in the United States of America

ISBN 9781609576844

All rights reserved solely by the author. The author guarantees all contents are original and do not infringe upon the legal rights of any other person or work. No part of this book may be reproduced in any form without the permission of the author. The views expressed in this book are not necessarily those of the publisher.

www.xulonpress.com

Samantha Weston, a young girl raised in Swanton, Ohio, takes you on a trip through her life as she and her family, face many trials and tribulations in their everyday lives. Her hopes and dreams become apparent as she travels through her life with the love of her family and friends alongside her. All of this proving that dreams really can come true if you believe in yourself and have faith in a higher power!

I would like to dedicate this book to my Mom, who has always been there for me. Through the years, during good times or bad, my Mom has been my biggest fan and I thank her for her guidance. This one's for you, Mom! Thank you and I love you!

    EVELYN

I would like to acknowledge a few people who have supported me through this venture. Thank you first of all to my husband, Kevin, for keeping his faith in me through this long journey. Thanks also to my daughter, Rachel, for helping me to type this book. A thank you to my nephew, Damon, for the wonderful illustrations that he drew for me! And thanks to my sister, Amy, for her suggestions for the format of the book. And to the rest of my extended family, thank you all for your words of encouragement. You all know who you are!

Thank you each and every one of you for your support and love!

    EVELYN

Chapter one

Soft, Classical music played over the speakers, as they made their way down the hallway, from the dressing room, where she had gotten ready and calmed her nerves. Samantha's heart skipped a beat as she walked with her father, through the doors of the Church sanctuary. She had dreamed of this day since she had been a little girl and now, it was here. And it couldn't be more perfect!

The roses that Samantha had chosen, adorned the aisles of the Church, and her Maid of Honor and Bridesmaids were beautiful in the periwinkle Chiffon dresses that they had agreed upon together. Yes, everything was perfect, although somehow Samantha was unable to see her Groom! She blinked her eyes and looked again but still could not see the face of the man that she was about to marry.

Then, a distant voice called to her, saying, "Samantha, you'll be late for school if you don't get out of bed! Once again, she had been awakened from her wedding dream, as had happened many times before...

Samantha hurried to get dressed and ready for another day at school. Mom had packed Samantha and her brothers a sack lunch, as she did every day, for each of them. Samantha hoped that Mom had put some of her delicious home-made cookies in her lunch, as she had the most insatiable 'Sweet Tooth' these days!

As she waited for the School bus with her brothers, Samantha hoped that her friend, Melissa had saved her a seat next to her. She couldn't wait to tell Melissa about her dream last night!

The bus driver hurried them all aboard and Samantha found that her friend had not rode the bus that morning, so she settled in next to Joey, her next door neighbor.

Once at school, Samantha put her lunch and gym clothes inside the locker she shared with Susan, another classmate. The Sixth Grade Wing, as they called it, was just a couple of seconds away from her classroom, where Miss Jones sat at her desk, waiting for everyone to take their seats. Samantha was called on first to solve the math equation on the chalkboard.

She cringed when she heard her name called and hesitantly walked to the front of the room to solve the math problem. You see, Samantha hated math and was embarrassed to go in front of her class to solve a math problem. She almost always got the answer wrong and was snickered at because of it. Oh, why did Miss Jones call on her so often when she knew that Samantha struggled to understand math? Could it be that Samantha's teacher was building Self-Esteem, without her even knowing it?

Samantha Annette Weston was born to her parents, William and Cindy, on July 13, 1965, at Tanner Memorial Hospital in Swanton, Ohio. Her two brothers, Scott and Charles, were not very happy that they had a new baby sister. They much rather would have liked a baby brother instead. They each took a turn looking at Samantha's wrinkled little face and tiny body and both decided she wasn't so bad after all! She'd be O.K. for them to tease. As soon as she could say their names, the fun would begin!

When Samantha got home from school, she changed into her play clothes, as Mom called them. She then went outside to do her afternoon chores. Feeding the chickens and gathering the eggs didn't take long at all, so Samantha decided to look for wildflowers for her Mom. Cindy enjoyed the flowers that Samantha brought for the Supper table and thanked her daughter for the beautiful bouquet that she had found. Her mother wasn't surprised when Samantha told her how her brothers had hid in the fencerow and thrown pebbles at her. But Samantha wasn't afraid of those little monsters!

Growing up on a farm in Southern Ohio, Samantha and her brothers enjoyed fresh vegetables from the garden, which Mom canned for the long months of winter. Sometimes, Mom would let Samantha help when she made fresh jam, and of course, the kids always got to try a sample of the sweet treat!

Samantha's Mom had made fried chicken and mashed potatoes and gravy for their supper. Everyone feasted on the delicious meal before doing their homework and getting ready for bed.

Sometimes, Dad stayed late, working in the fields, so Mom saved some supper to warm up for him later, when he came inside for the night. Mom was thoughtful that way. She wouldn't let anyone go hungry, not even the friends who visited the house. Mostly, the kids that lived in the city, who enjoyed the fresh country air and appreciated the many acres to romp around on, Mom always fed them too!

Samantha was in the locker room getting ready for Gym class, when she overheard some of the girls talking about the 'S' word. She thought to herself how gross it sounded, when the other girls tried to explain the basics to her. You see, Samantha's Mom had simply said that it was something that married couples do in private' and that left Samantha wondering exactly what it was all about!

Later that afternoon, Samantha talked with her friend, Melissa about this 'S' word talk. But Melissa didn't know much more than she did. Oh well, one day they would both figure it all out and it would all make sense. In the meantime, Samantha's mother was planning her birthday party and she had told her that she could invite five of her friends. A sleep-over was being planned, that is, if Samantha agreed that it would be a great idea to have five screaming girls in her bedroom for a night. She decided that she wouldn't invite Jody because she thought she was 'All that and a Bag of chips'. And Samantha didn't want Jody to ruin her Birthday party. So she made her list of five good friends and gave it to her Mom, so she could address the party invitations.

A few weeks had passed since school was over for the year and summer vacation had begun. This meant that the big Birthday party was next week. Samantha couldn't wait until she turned '12', because she had asked for a new bicycle for her birthday. The old one she had was a 'Hand-me-Down' from a friend and it had seen better days.

Saturday, July 13th, had finally arrived and Samantha couldn't be happier! She happily helped her mother get the party decorations put up. Samantha had asked for pizza and pop, and of course, Mom's delicious Home-made birthday cake! It would surely be the best weekend of the whole summer!

That is, until her Mom received a phone call from Melissa's Mom, saying that Melissa had the chicken pox and wouldn't be able to come to Samantha's party. Samantha was sad that Melissa would miss her party, but thought she would take her some cake later on.

Friends started arriving around 12:45 P.M., so Samantha made sure to greet each one of them. She thanked them all for coming to her Birthday party. Manners always were important to Samantha, as she and her brothers were taught to use them very young.

The party turned out to be a "Blast' and Samantha received a lot of gifts that day. One of which was her brand new bike from Mom and Dad! It was a beauty!! The color was purple and it had a pretty pink, basket on the front for her treasures. What a wonderful day it had been. Samantha could hardly take it all in!

She was exhausted, so it didn't take long for to fall asleep in her cozy, comfortable twin bed. She quickly fell into a deep sleep and once again, her dreams of her Wedding Day were a big part of her evening's sleep. Samantha hadn't told anyone about her repetitive dreams, except her good friend, Melissa. Samantha knew that her friend would not blab to others about it.

Undoubtedly, Samantha was a little on the chubby side, unlike a lot of girls in her class at school. Most were thin, athletic and of course, quite popular.

Sometimes, she struggled to make new friends but she knew for sure that her true friends would all stick by her, no matter what came their way. Besides, so-called popularity surely didn't make a person. Samantha's Mom had always told her that 'Beauty comes from the Inside". So, Samantha was O.K. with herself and her good friends.

Chapter two

The fall came and went, as well as the Holidays. But it was still winter in Southern Ohio, much to Samantha's delight. She and her brothers loved to go sledding in one of the fields on their property. One that was home to one of the best sledding hills around!

They each took a turn on the aluminum snow saucer or sometimes they rode all together on the three person toboggan. It was so much fun that none of them minded that they were soaked to the skin . They would warm up by the wood stove when they got home and Mom would make them each a mug of hot cocoa too.

'Oh, those were the days', Samantha said to Melissa as they sat and reminisced over lunch in the cafeteria. It seemed like yesterday that they were in grade school, and now they were freshman in High School! As they were talking, their friend, Tom, came over and sat down with them for a moment. 'Will either of you be trying out for the school musical'? Tom asked the two friends.' I'm going to try out at the auditorium today at 5:30'. The girls looked at one another and in unison, answered Tom with, 'I don't think so'. He knew that both girls were beautiful singers and that they both stood a good chance of 'Making the Cut', as they called it.

'I don't know', said Samantha. 'I get a little nervous in front of a crowd of people'. Melissa then claimed that she was much too busy to join them at try-outs, but wished them both the best of luck. Finally, Samantha agreed to go to try-outs with Tom that afternoon. 'I've got to go to class' Melissa told them, as she gathered her books and left them at the small table near the drinking fountain.

At try-outs that afternoon, Samantha was quite nervous but somehow pulled it together long enough to calm her stomach butterflies. She chewed her fingernail as she waited for her turn on stage. She had done a good job on the song that she had chosen, and she was so proud of herself! Her thoughts quickly changed once Tom took his turn on stage. Something inside of her seemed to awaken as she heard him sing. It was so beautiful!!

Why hadn't she heard him sing before? Samantha thought to herself. All she could think was that she wanted to hear him sing again! It was unbelievable how Tom's singing voice made her feel! In a word, Amazing!!!

It was another two weeks before anyone knew whether or not they had been chosen to be in the school musical. The music director had told them that the list would be posted in the lobby at the auditorium, on Wednesday afternoon. 'I can't stand the wait', Samantha told Melissa while they waited in the cafeteria line for lunch. 'Why does it take so long for them to decide'? Melissa just shook her head and told Samantha to settle down and relax. And soon enough, she would know the results of Try-Outs.

After algebra class, Samantha hurried to the theatre lobby to see if 'The List' had been posted yet. 'Guys and Dolls' would begin in September this year and the excitement was indescribable, especially for Samantha. As she entered the lobby, she could hear the muffled sounds of both happiness and disappointment as each person looked for their name on the Cast list. Samantha slowly made her way through the crowd to search at last for her own name.

She leapt for joy, when indeed she did see her name on the list. And much to her surprise, she had taken the lead female role!! Tom's name was of course on the list alongside hers, as the male lead role. Samantha just about fainted to think that she would be in the same musical with Tom. She frantically searched for her friend, Melissa to tell her the good news.

Rehearsals were scheduled to start next Tuesday. Samantha could already feel a case of nervousness edging it's way into her body. She hurried outside to wait for her mother to pick her up, all the while thinking about her debut on the big stage, in a couple of months!

Tom looked up from his script as Samantha called his name. She had just arrived at play rehearsal in the nick of time. She was confident that she could master this role, if she worked hard and studied her lines often. 'Are you ready young lady'? Tom asked as she sat down next to him, script in hand. She answered him with, 'Yes, I believe I'm ready as I'll ever be'. She looked into Tom's deep blue eyes and felt that 'fuzzy' feeling again, as if he had sang the question to her.

Why was she so entranced by his presence? And why was she so comfortable to be near him? Samantha set aside her 'mushy' feelings and seriously thought about her lines. An answer to her questions would surely come to her but not as quickly as she would have liked.

After a long day of school, rehearsals and homework, Samantha was exhausted. She told her parents 'Good Night' and went upstairs to get ready for bed. She fell asleep pondering the day's events. And those beautiful notes that Tom had sang at rehearsal that day.

It had been weeks since the cast of 'Guys and Dolls', had begun rehearsing. The final Dress Rehearsal was next Thursday. Samantha was a nervous wreck but knew that the show would be a 'Hit' with the audiences. Tom and Samantha had rehearsed their lines together a few times over coffee at the local 'Café'. Samantha had grown very fond of Tom's company, over these last few weeks. He seemed so kind and sweet, she felt giddy sometimes, when she was with him. She hoped he didn't notice too much!

Today was Thursday, September 5th, and it was the night of the Dress Rehearsal at Coolidge High School. She smiled as she thought about how handsome Tom looked in his stage costumes.

Samantha left her last class for the day and headed towards her locker to gather her homework. Melissa was there waiting for her when she got there. Melissa seemed a little uptight about something, so Samantha asked her friend what was wrong. Her best friend proceeded to tell her that she and her family would be moving, after Thanksgiving. Melissa's Dad had been re-located to Oregon for his job as an Engineer.

This meant that Melissa's family would be moving before the Christmas Holiday! The girls hugged one another and sobbed as they each made a pact to never forget the other, and to always stay in touch with each other, whether by phone or by mail. This was not a good day for Melissa to be telling Samantha that she had to move away! What with the big Dress Rehearsal tonight, Samantha had to remain focused on the show and nothing else!!

Chapter three

The events of the past year brought both happiness and sadness to Samantha's thoughts. But she always remembered that everything happened for a reason. Whether or not we understood it all, things always had a way of working out. Samantha's Mom, Cindy had always told her children, 'No matter what happens in our lives, we will one day realize why we all go through these rough times'.

Samantha smiled as she stepped out of the dressing room and made her way backstage. Dress Rehearsal was about to begin and everyone was ready to go onstage. Samantha breathed a sigh of relief as she saw fellow cast members, also anxiously awaiting the start of the show. The pressure to do your very best, to remember your lines and to sing on cue, were on everyone's mind.

Samantha could hardly wait for this night to be over. Her nerves were beginning to get the best of her! A wink from Tom before the curtains opened seemed to calm her down some but the butterflies were still fluttering inside her belly!! When the show finally began, time seemed to fly and before Samantha knew it, the crowd was applauding. The cast had done a great job and a standing ovation was in order!! Their hard work and determination had paid off. And the director couldn't be happier for them!

Samantha was talking with other cast members after the show, when Tom walked over to congratulate her on a job 'well-done'. She thanked him for his compliment, then also told him what a great job he, himself had done. Tom said his 'good job' to all the others before pulling Samantha aside, to see if she had plans for Saturday. There was a new movie opening at the theatre downtown and he wanted to ask Samantha to go with him to it.

Samantha thought about her parent's rule about dating. She wouldn't be '16' until next summer, so she had to decline Tom's offer on the movie. Samantha graciously thanked Tom for the invitation and told him of her parent's rule. 'It's O.K.', Tom told her. I understand that you need to follow the rules. 'I myself have rules at my house also', Tom replied. The two said their good-byes and went on their separate ways to their homes.

As Samantha expected, her parents said 'No' to a movie with Tom. Maybe they could all get together for some ice cream or something, one day, she thought. After two weeks of performances, the musical production of 'Guys and Dolls' was finished. And everyone breathed a sigh of relief after the final show! The director, Mrs. Brown, complimented the whole cast on a 'job well done'. She also mentioned Try-Outs for the next school musical, 'Oklahoma'.

Samantha rode home after the show with her family, who had supported her through all of the rehearsals and the script-reading. They all had taken their turns reading with her in order for her to learn her lines. Samantha's family took care to celebrate their accomplishments together and this was no exception!

The next few weeks, Samantha spent as much time studying as she could. The Mid-Term exams were coming up and she wanted to be prepared. Samantha and Melissa often studied together so they could quiz one another. Sometimes, they chatted about the boys they thought were cute.

Of course, Tom's name was mentioned in their conversations. Melissa now knew more about this boy that her friend was smitten by! Those 'funny' feelings were brought up and neither one knew what they meant for sure. Melissa thought that it might be Samantha's hormones kicking in. She had heard her Mother say that happens when you're 'infatuated' with someone. 'My mom said that's how I am around our neighbor kid, Shawn. 'But I told her that he's a 'goof', Melissa said.

Samantha smiled at her friend and knew just how she felt! Boys were strange creatures. That was for sure. But Samantha didn't think that Tom was so bad. Not bad at all!

Melissa and Samantha spent many hours together because in just a couple of months, Melissa would be moving to Oregon with her family. Samantha would miss Melissa dearly but hoped they would still keep in touch. The girls eventually would say their 'good-byes' and sob once again. It was so hard to have your best friend move away from you! Samantha wasn't sure that she could stand it!!

But somehow the two friends would pull it together and build their friendship stronger than it had ever been. This wasn't the first time that a friend would move from Swanton. Samantha remembered in Grade School, another friend that had moved away from Swanton. She remembered a girl named Betty and wondered what ever had happened to her???

Chapter four

William and Cindy had invited some guests over for their annual Halloween party.
Everyone was asked to dress up and most of the guests conformed to the rule.

Samantha's parents chose 'Frankenstein' and 'Bride of Frankenstein'. Samantha watched in awe as the two of them walked into the kitchen. The resemblance was uncanny!! Samantha excused herself so she too could change into her own costume for the party. 'Little Red Riding Hood' had been Samantha's choice for the festivities.

The Halloween Party was a hit with all of the guests. What with the 'Bat Wing Dip' and the 'Bloody Punch', William and Cindy's guests were treated to a smorgasbord of tasty treats that evening. And the costumes were a 'hoot', as one by one, the guests paraded through the living room for the costume contest. There was a Queen, a Gypsy and even a Court Jester! Samantha's favorite was the man dressed as a woman. What a great costume! What a good time everyone had that night, even Samantha!!

It would soon be the Holidays, so fall was turning away as quickly as it had come, to the small town of Swanton. And it's many residents who welcomed the harvest season!

Samantha awoke to the birds singing, outside of her bedroom window. Time had flown and of course, winter had fallen on the farm. Samantha thought how cheerful the birds sounded, as if it were the first day of spring! Yet, it was already the middle of December!! Samantha was surprised at the amount of snow that had fallen during the night! She hurried to get out of bed to get ready for the big day ahead.

Melissa was in town for the weekend. She and Samantha were planning to shop for some Christmas gifts, after getting some lunch at the mall. Cindy had agreed to drop the girls off at the shopping plaza, as long as they were ready to be picked up by 4:00 P.M. Cindy gave Melissa an extra $20.00, just in case she found something for her brothers for Christmas.

Samantha and Melissa hadn't seen each other since Melissa had moved away in November. It was now the middle of December, and the two girls had plenty to talk about! There was no time to be wasted on mindless chatter, so the girls cut to the chase and discussed all of the important things in their lives. Their lunches had consisted of submarine sandwiches and soda pop. This suited the both of them just fine. They had more important things to think about!

The two friends had scoured the mall stores, searching for that special gift, for everyone on their lists. Many a bargain had been found by the two 'spindrift' shoppers. And both were excited to get back home to sort through their treasures. It was so good to see Melissa that Samantha didn't want the day to end. But unfortunately, Melissa couldn't stay for long in Ohio. Her Dad needed to get back to his new job in Oregon and their new life there!

Earlier, Melissa had mentioned her new boyfriend, Joshua. Samantha was surprised that Melissa's parents allowed her to date at her young age. Samantha knew that her friend was most definitely not ready to date anyone seriously. But the way that Melissa talked, the two had been dating for a couple of months already! Melissa had beamed when she talked about Joshua. But Samantha wondered about the relationship and just how serious it was. This relationship sounded as if it might be headed for trouble! And Samantha was worried for her friend.

Melissa had told Samantha that she and Joshua had been discussing a more serious relationship. Samantha cringed at the thought because her friend was way too young for this type of seriousness with a boy!! Melissa had been surprised to hear Samantha's response after she had told her about Joshua. Her friend had told her, 'You two are getting way too close'! 'That's my honest opinion on the situation', Samantha told Melissa. Immediately, Samantha had asked Melissa to change the subject!

Melissa and her family left to go back to Oregon that Sunday. As Samantha hugged her friend 'good-bye', she whispered in Melissa's ear to 'Be careful in this situation with Joshua'. Samantha then said 'good-bye' to everyone as they got into their family car. 'Have a safe trip', Samantha whispered as they drove off. Samantha hoped her friend knew that she was only looking out for her.

Christmas was just weeks away and the 'Weston's were busy getting the house ready for the Holidays, and baking the traditional 'goodies' that came along with preparations for Christmas. Cindy and Samantha enjoyed their time in the kitchen, working to get cookies made for the weeks ahead. Sampling was allowed, as long as it was in moderation.

Later that evening after supper, Cindy asked Samantha to help wrap some gifts. She quickly agreed to help so that they could put them under the Christmas tree. The excitement was too much! Samantha loved the Holidays, simply for the festive atmosphere around the farmhouse. Everything glistened with shimmer and shine. It was impossible for Samantha to quit smiling. Could it be that part of the excitement was the beautifully wrapped gift under the Christmas tree, that had Samantha's name on it?

No matter, it was a happy time of year at Samantha's house and nothing could change the mood.

Everyone was looking forward to the big Christmas dinner that Cindy cooked each year. This was a feast beyond imagination! And nobody left the table hungry either. The only thing left to wish for this Christmas, was snow, and lots of it! Samantha's heart was so full of happiness she thought it just might burst out of her chest!!

Samantha and her brothers had pooled their money together in order to get their parents a gift. They had chosen a new record player for William and Cindy. It was high time that their old one become 'history'. A new record album of "Swing' music had also been selected, to go along with the record player. The siblings hoped the parents would appreciate the thought they had put into their gifts.

Samantha looked ahead to the New Year, '1980', and realized that she would turn '15' years old next summer. This also meant she would be one year closer to '16', and quite possibly, to being old enough to 'date'. Samantha wondered to herself if Tom would still be interested in asking her out when she was old enough? What would she do if he wasn't?

Chapter five

The bitter January winds blew through the tiny town of Swanton that winter. Samantha wished for spring to arrive and soon! She bundled up to go outside to do her afternoon chores. She hurried to the chicken coop to get herself out of the wind. 'Lord, have mercy', she said, as she shut the door behind her. Samantha couldn't remember the winter ever being this cold! She gathered the eggs and checked the small door, to see that it was latched good and tight. No nasty varmints were going to get into this hen house, if Samantha had anything to say about it!!

Samantha made her way back to the house. Once inside, she hung her wet clothes up on the hooks that her Dad had made, just for that purpose. Sloppy, wet clothes were not allowed to be strewn all over the 'mud room', so Samantha made sure to follow the house rules. Supper was ready, so the Weston family sat down to eat after a long winter's day at the farm. These were the times when everyone could catch up on the affairs of the day, and bond as a family.

Although Charles and Scott were older, Samantha still was curious about their lives as 'Upper classmen', at her school. The boys weren't too keen on telling their little sister any information about their personal lives with their friends and the like, so she was left 'in the dark' about the two of them! So be it! Samantha was happy just to be a part of a close-knit family just the same. Even if her brothers wouldn't give out any tidbits of info on their lives.

As Samantha got ready for school the next morning, she took a moment to look at herself in the mirror. She noticed that she was starting to 'slim down' a bit and was beginning to get a 'womanly' figure. She smiled to herself as she brushed her teeth. Samantha had begun getting her 'monthly visitor', last summer, but it wasn't as bad as everyone had talked.

Quite pleased with herself, Samantha went downstairs for some breakfast. The school bus would be here shortly, so she hurried to make some toast and peanut butter, one of her favorites! Her brothers had already left, as Scott had his own truck. He didn't offer to give Samantha a ride to school because that wasn't 'cool'. She didn't mind riding the bus. It gave her the chance to talk with her friends, anyway. Besides, the goofy looking truck that Scott drove wasn't exactly Samantha's choice for a ride!

Spring had finally arrived again and there was a rare stillness in the air, as Samantha waited for the school bus. The birds seemed to be singing extra loudly today too! As she climbed onto the bus voices carried her to another time, when it was the first day of 'kindergarten'. Both nervous and excited, Samantha had awaited that day, for what seemed like forever to a five year old! She was brought back to reality by the bus driver, shouting to her to 'take a seat, Miss Weston'. Samantha sat down and thought about her friend, Melissa in Oregon. She missed her best friend and wished that she hadn't moved so far away!

Samantha's parents would be celebrating their '25th' Wedding Anniversary, this year. Some friends of theirs were planning a surprise party for them. Samantha had been asked by Cindy's friend, Linda, for some names and addresses of family and friends. Samantha was happy to help. The fun part was trying to get the information without Cindy and William finding out! But nonetheless, Samantha would do what she had been asked to do.

As she walked up the road to Linda's house, Samantha hoped that she hadn't forgotten anyone on her list of guests. When she arrived at Linda's house, she rang the doorbell and waited. When nobody came to the door, she tried the handle and found the house was unlocked. She called out as she stepped inside, and when she didn't get any response, decided to leave the list on the dining room table for Linda. As Samantha crossed the foyer into the dining room, she could hear noises coming from upstairs.

She thought to herself that maybe, Linda was on the phone or something. As Samantha approached the stairway, the laughter became louder. She crept up the steps ever so quietly, as not to disturb Linda in case she was talking on the phone. Much to Samantha's surprise, it was not Linda in her bedroom at all. It was Linda's daughter, Susie, in her mother's bedroom, smoking cigarettes and talking on the phone. As quickly as she had crept upstairs, Samantha quietly snuck back down them. She didn't want Susie to know that she had been there!

Cigarettes! Samantha cringed at the thought of Susie smoking. Not only in her mother's room, but smoking her mother's cigarettes too! What would Linda think to see her daughter smoking?? As she hurried back home, Samantha wondered if she should tell someone about it. The surprising part about this whole scene was that Susie was only fourteen!! She just had to tell someone about this!

That evening, after supper dishes had been washed, Samantha asked her mother if she could talk with her privately. Cindy agreed, so the two went into the living room to talk. Samantha told her mother what she had witnessed, that afternoon. 'Mom, can you please tell Linda about this'? Samantha pleaded with her mother, as if she would burst into tears at any second. 'Yes, Samantha, I will talk with Linda for you', 'But why on earth were you at Linda's house in the first place'? Cindy asked her daughter.

Samantha thought quickly of a lame excuse, about a project for school, that she thought Linda might be able to help her with. Cindy seemed to accept the reason that Samantha so quickly made up! Whew! Samantha took a deep breath and realized that she could have almost, 'let the cat out of the bag', on this one! But the main thing was, that Cindy would speak with Linda about Susie's smoking habit and this was very important!! The surprise had been kept a secret, thanks to Samantha's little 'white lie'.

'I really miss you, Samantha', Melissa told her over the phone that evening. 'I miss you too, Melissa', she responded to her friend. There was something in Melissa's voice that made Samantha feel somewhat uneasy. Samantha asked her friend what was bothering her, and was somehow, not surprised by her answer. 'Joshua and I almost crossed 'the line' last week, Samantha', Melissa confessed to her friend. 'What made you change your mind, Melissa'?

Samantha asked her. 'I thought about what you would think about it and I told Joshua that I'm just not ready'.

'You have always been my best friend, Samantha' and I don't want anything to change that', Melissa confessed. Samantha told Melissa she had made the right choice and commended her for it. 'We are too young to be burdened with 'adult' choices', Samantha told her friend. 'Besides, why would we want to go against what we've been taught'? 'I'm proud of you for standing your ground with Joshua'. Melissa was relieved to hear her friend's response and breathed a sigh of relief.

The friends talked for a little while longer, before saying 'good-night'. Samantha was way past 'tired' tonight, so sleep was a welcome friend that night. At any rate, sleep came that night, along with the distant dream of a wedding, a far-off dream that Samantha wondered would ever come true…

Chapter six

The surprise Anniversary party for Cindy and William went off 'without a hitch'. The couple couldn't have been more surprised! Linda was thankful to have friends like the Westons. And she was honored to throw this party for the two of them. They deserved this special evening, honoring the love they had shared for many years.

The children had their own festivities, downstairs in the basement. Linda had prepared some 'kid friendly' foods for them all to enjoy. There also was 'Twister', some movies and of course, 'Atari', a favorite at the 'Michaels' house. A good time was had by everyone, even the family dog, 'Shirley'!

It had been a very long day, so the Westons thanked Linda for her hospitality, and headed back home for the night. As they all walked towards home, Cindy inquired of Samantha about keeping the secret of the party from them. 'I just kept telling myself that I couldn't tell anyone'. 'It was the hardest thing to keep quiet about', she told her mother. Cindy thanked Samantha for helping to make this a 'night to remember'.

Samantha had enjoyed the secret planning of the big party. Linda had been nice to ask her to help with the preparations. Samantha appreciated her parents and thought it would be the least she could do to help Linda out.

The summer had gone by quickly, once again. Samantha thought about how they flew by, now that she was growing up, and on her way to being a sophomore at school this year. She sat down at the breakfast table with her Dad. Samantha then asked about the time when he himself was her age. William thought for a moment then began to tell Samantha about his two best friends in High School.

Their names were Bart and Clyde. And what the three of them enjoyed the most was setting off 'bottle rockets' for fun.

William proceeded to speak about the time when the three friends experimented with several types of materials, to fuel their rockets. It turned out that Clyde ended up getting second and third degree burns real bad on his face and neck. 'I'll never forget that day', William told his daughter. It seemed as if it hurt William, to discuss the painful memory of that day. Samantha asked her Dad 'What makes boys so careless'? William replied with, 'It's just in their nature, Samantha'.

William then excused himself from the table, in order to go to the barn, to do the chores. Samantha hugged her Dad before he went outside for the morning routine. She then grabbed her lunch off the kitchen counter, called to her mother, 'I Love You' then went outside to wait for the school bus. Samantha then realized that her mother had not answered her. She ran back inside the house to see that Cindy was alright.

She found Cindy in the bathroom, trying to put on some make-up. It seemed that she was having a hard time covering up the fact that she had been crying. She hadn't wanted Samantha to see her like this! Samantha asked her mother what was wrong. Cindy asked Samantha to sit with her on the bed, so they could talk for a while. It seemed that William was sick, very sick. Cindy took Samantha's hand in hers and mustered enough strength to tell about her dad's illness.

Samantha saw her mother falter over her words and wondered just how serious this situation was. A million thoughts were going through Samantha's mind, all at once! Oh, how were they all going to get through this?? Samantha asked her mother if her brothers knew about their Dad's sickness. 'Yes, your brothers know', 'but I wanted to tell you myself'. It seemed that William had not felt well for a while now. 'I'm sorry', Samantha said to her mother, as the two embraced one another.

This was going to be a true test of her Dad's strength and courage, but Samantha knew that the 'Good Lord' did not put more on your shoulders, than what you could bear on your own! The test results had found that William had cancer of the prostate, a part of the male anatomy. Cindy had also told Samantha that her Dad would begin 'Chemo-therapy', next week. This all seemed like a bad dream to Samantha. Why was this happening? And why was it happening to her Dad?

Samantha and her mother embraced once again then sobbed together, there in the bedroom. A few more details were explained to Samantha, so that she might better understand her Dad's sickness. Samantha once again, hugged her mother, then whispered in her ear that, 'We all need to be strong for Dad'. Cindy agreed with her young daughter. 'I'll call the school office for you', 'so you can be excused for the day', Cindy told Samantha. 'Let's not let Dad know that we've been crying', O.K. Mom'? Cindy agreed to put a smile on for William's sake.

Cindy called the school for her daughter then put on some tea for them. Dad came in from the barn a short while later and knew that Cindy had told Samantha the news. The look on his daughter's face said it all. The sadness in her eyes was heart-breaking. William hugged Samantha and promised her that he would do everything that the doctors told him. No matter what!! Samantha hugged her Dad and sobbed uncontrollably. It was obvious how this had affected her.

William assured his daughter that this was just a 'bump in the road', and he was going to fight for his life, no matter what it took. Even if it took everything that he had in him, he would not give up! Samantha told him how much she loved him then sat down again to her cup of tea. The three of them held one another, as Cindy said a prayer for William. Every bit of help would be needed to pull through something like this! Faith would play a big role in William's care and healing. And the Weston Family had plenty to hold onto!

Samantha hugged both her parents and let them each know how very much she loved each of them. 'We'll get through this', Samantha told them, as she went upstairs to lie down. This had been a trying morning for her and she needed a rest. Maybe just a short nap would help her digest all that she had learned today.

William had taken several chemo-therapy treatments since September. He really wasn't feeling too bad at this point. Considering all that he had been through in the past two months, he felt pretty good. Samantha prayed for her Dad's health, every night before she went to bed. And Samantha prayed for her mother also. She prayed for the strength that Cindy would need for the long road ahead, and for the wisdom to keep her family calm through all of this.

Sometimes, Samantha found it real hard to put on a smiling face, because her Dad looked so sad and forlorn. This sickness had taken a toll on William and it showed on his face. Nothing in his life could have prepared him for this life-changing chapter. And he felt the strain that this was putting on his family! He prayed that God would help him to stay strong for his family. They surely weren't ready to deal with such a major health matter, not right now.

William had begun to lose some weight because of the 'chemo-therapy' treatments. He simply did not feel like eating most of the time. His appetite had pretty much left him, about a month ago. He tried to eat what the family ate, but it just wasn't working out for him. Cindy tried to prepare meals that the whole family could enjoy and nobody complained. If it meant that Dad could sit with them during meals, the kids didn't care at all.

Scott and Charles were helping more now with chores and Samantha tried helping the best that she could. Everyone was pitching in and helping to get things done. William wasn't allowed to go to the barn by himself now and this made him feel guilty. His sons were stepping up and taking on more responsibility. The boys didn't mind helping out, it seemed to be the right thing to do, during their Dad's time of need.

Friends stopped by often, to see if there was anything that they could help out with. Cindy graciously told them, 'No thank-you' and told them all that they were alright. Always the pillar of the family, Cindy took each day as it came, and tried to make the best of it, for William's sake. Samantha admired her mother for her strength. She could only hope that one day she would follow in her footsteps!

Samantha sat down at her small desk and proceeded to write a letter to her friend, Melissa. She wanted to let her know about her Dad's condition. Samantha was careful not to go into too much detail, so as not to scare Melissa. Samantha knew that Melissa's Mother also had some health issues herself. When the girls were young, Carol had been diagnosed with diabetes. It had been a long road, getting her healthy again, but she had persevered through it all.

After just a little bit more chit-chat, Samantha told Melissa 'good-bye', and signed her name to her letter. She then went to tell her parents 'good-night', then brushed her teeth and crawled into her bed. But not before saying her prayers. Samantha prayed each night for her Dad, without fail! It was the least that she could do, if it meant that he may get better and beat this disease!!

Samantha thought about her Dad's illness for a moment and wondered to herself, why did this type of thing happen to good people? She closed her eyes and wished this horrible sickness would just go away from her Dad. But in her heart, she knew that it was going to take more than just wishing, to be rid of this awful thing!

Chapter seven

This week on Thursday, Cindy would take William to meet with an Oncologist, at the Cancer Center in downtown Finley. The appointment was during school hours, so Samantha and her brothers would have to wait until they got home, to find out about William's progress.

Samantha saw Tom in the hallway after algebra class. He asked her how her Dad was doing. It had been a few weeks since Samantha had talked to Tom, and she felt that crazy, funny feeling, coming over her again. Samantha politely told Tom of her Dad's condition then thanked him for asking. She wasn't expecting what happened next! Tom drew Samantha close and hugged her tight. 'If you need anything, please let me know, Samantha', Tom told her. 'I will be happy to help in any way that I can'.

'Thank-you Tom', Samantha responded. 'You are very sweet', she told him, as he hurried to his next class. Samantha was stunned, but not surprised at Tom's actions. He was a compassionate guy and was not afraid to show his feelings. Not at all, especially around Samantha! She hurried to her history class, just as the bell rang. Samantha was half listening to the teacher, as he babbled on about some General in some war or something.

She couldn't think about anything much except the hug that Tom had given her earlier. She was jolted back to reality by the bell for class to end. It surely couldn't have rung at a better time. Samantha wanted to get home to see about her Dad. It was the most important thing on her mind right now, so she hurried outside to catch the bus. It was Samantha's turn to help with supper tonight, so she needed to help her Mom as soon as she was told of William's condition.

The news from the Oncologist was not good. The cancer had spread to William's colon and some of his other vital organs. The doctors would need to 'step-up' the treatments, to Radiation, once a week for six weeks. They hoped that these treatments would help to target the cancer that was quickly spreading through William's body.

Everyone managed to keep busy in the work at the farm. William was unable to go to the barn at all now. His treatments had left him weak and unable to stand for any amount of time. Scott and Charles took care of the cattle and the crops, while Cindy and Samantha handled some of the other chores at the barn. William tried to put a smile on when his family was around, but it seemed to be getting harder for him to do.

This cancer had taken a toll on William, not only physically, but mentally also. And the pain of this ordeal was beginning to show on his face! At supper that evening, William spoke to everyone about the farm and what they should do if something were to happen to him. In disbelief, the family listened to William, although none of them were ready for this type of talk. Not just yet! They had all agreed to do their parts in order to keep the farm going. But at this point, it was not clear, just how soon they might be on their own, without William's guiding hand.

Supper dishes had been washed and it was time to sit together as a family to watch 'Magnum P.I.', a favorite show of the family. Dad really liked the guy who played the character of 'Higgins', on the hit show. After the show was over, they all said their 'good-nights' and went off to their rooms for the night. It had been another long day and everyone was ready for bed that night.

The next few days were spent getting the wheat combined and the straw baled. This had to be done while the weather was dry, so there was no time to be wasted. William rode along inside the combine with Charles to make sure that everything went well. He felt that he was helping somewhat, even though he needed help getting in and out of the combine. Charles was glad to spend time with his Dad. He felt a lump grow in his throat when he thought what it would be like without his Dad around.

Charles wasn't the type to feel sorry for himself but he didn't want to lose his Dad. He had been such a great role model to him. The thought of not having him around just about broke his heart.

Charles cleared his mind and got back to the task at hand. The task of getting the rest of the wheat combined.

Fall harvest was always a busy time for Cindy and Samantha. It was canning season and Samantha knew that it was her job to help her Mom in the kitchen. And she gladly obliged. It wouldn't be long before Thanksgiving, so the Weston women made sure to prepare plenty of vegetables for the season ahead. Cindy's expertise in canning was amazing to Samantha. Her knowledge about each type of vegetable was surprising!

Samantha could only hope that she too, could one day teach her children the same things that her Mom had taught her. When the canning was done, the women cleaned the kitchen then sat down to rest for a moment. Samantha asked her Mother, 'Mom, how are we going to get by without Dad'? Cindy looked at her daughter and told her, 'Honey, we will do the best we can'. 'It's going to be alright', she told her.

Samantha's mind was put at ease, at least for the moment. But she still kept thinking about it. She really couldn't imagine life without her Dad around! Samantha tried to set those thoughts aside, so she could go outside to do her chores.

That evening, Samantha sat in her room doing her homework. She had an Algebra test the next day, so she needed to study hard. While she worked, she listened to her radio. A new song played on the station she was tuned into. The name of the song was, 'Magic', and it was sung by Olivia Newton John. An artist in her own right, Samantha appreciated a song with a good melody. 'What a great song', Samantha said to herself.

It seemed to be getting dark earlier these days, so Samantha turned her desk lamp on, so it would be easier for her to study. As darkness crept into her bedroom, Samantha thought about the winter months that were just around the corner. She shivered at the thought of having to wear her boots again! She really would much rather be barefoot. That was possibly the 'country girl' in her that made her dislike shoes so much!!

The next few weeks were grueling for William. The Radiation treatments had become more intense and more often than he had expected. Samantha had noticed that her Dad was looking terribly thin. And she had taken note that he was often, very tired. She felt so sorry for her Dad because he had been through all of this. Samantha's heart was heavy with sadness for William, but she tried not to let him see it in her eyes.

    Cindy had always told Samantha that everything happened for a reason, but she had a hard time believing that there was any type of reasoning behind this! It just wasn't fair for William to have to go through this kind of agony. Samantha could see that her Dad's pride had been shaken. He hated having everyone waiting on him, but there was so little he could do for himself now. William really did not have a choice in the matter anymore. Samantha did what she could to help make her Dad comfortable, but she knew that it just wasn't enough. Even though her Dad acted as if it was O.K., Samantha knew that this was crushing William inside!

Chapter eight

William's family did what they could to try and make life easier for him, as his health deteriorated before their eyes. Many nights, Cindy sat and thought about her life without her husband. She sometimes sat and cried herself to sleep, over the idea of being without him.

William and Cindy had met through a mutual friend. Their first date had been dinner and a movie together. Both were just twenty-one, when they met and they had been a couple ever since that first date. Cindy reflected back to their Wedding Day, and how happy they were. The new life they were about to begin together was all that William and Cindy cared about. And their future seemed as bright as those September stars that evening!

Their promise to one another, to stay together through 'thick and thin', had really brought the two of them much closer over their twenty-five years of marriage. A perfect match, that nobody could deny, was the union of William and Cindy, on that day so many years ago.

Cindy woke with a start, and realized that she had fallen asleep in the recliner once again. She had drifted off to sleep there, thinking about her family's future. She got up to make her way upstairs to her bed. The clock in the living room read twelve o'clock. Cindy had slept downstairs for two hours!! As she crawled into bed, she realized that one day, she may be sleeping here alone. She choked back a tear at the thought of it.

It was Saturday morning, so for a treat, Cindy was going to make pancakes and bacon for breakfast today. She climbed out of bed and went to the bathroom to get presentable, before going downstairs. A pot of coffee sounded delicious after last night's fitful sleep. When ready for the day, Cindy headed downstairs. As she reached the bottom landing, she caught A glimpse of William, lying in the kitchen doorway.

She let out a yell and ran to him. William was conscious but he was pale and his pulse was weak. Cindy helped him up unto a chair in the kitchen. She then called to her boys to help her get their Dad to the car. William was very ill and they needed to get him to the hospital. They called to Samantha to come downstairs right away! She was there in a flash and they hurried off to the emergency room.

When they arrived at the hospital, Charles ran inside and asked a nurse for a wheelchair for his Dad. She quickly grabbed one then she followed Charles outside. As soon as they entered the Emergency Room, William was whisked away to the Oncology unit, where the chief doctor on duty was waiting. The nurses worked quickly to make sure that William was comfortable. The doctor asked for William's records and ordered the nurses to check his vital signs for him.

One of the nurses asked Cindy to follow her to the front desk. She needed some information about William for the Insurance Company. Charles, Scott and Samantha sat and waited in the waiting room for their Mother. All were waiting for the condition of their 'beloved' Dad. Soon, Cindy came in to sit with her children, while they waited for word from the doctor.

While trying to be brave and strong for her children was hard for Cindy, she put forth a smile and reassured them that William was getting excellent care. It wasn't long before Doctor Hanson came in to speak with the family. The look on his face told them that William's condition was not good! As he sat down, Doctor Hansen discussed with the family what was happening with William.

The news, as the family expected, was not good. And at that moment, the reality of William's Cancer, hit them full force. Right in the middle of each of their hearts!! It seemed that William's organs were beginning to shut down. This meant that it would not be long before he would need 'life support' equipment. Cindy thanked the doctor and asked if she might have some time with her family.

For Cindy, it took everything in her to keep herself calm, while she discussed the decision whether or not to put William on 'life support'. Her children were very quiet as they thought for a while about the consequences of their decision. It was then decided, not to put William on 'life support' equipment. The tears came then as they shared a hug, there in the waiting room of the hospital. Before going to William's room, each of them got their bearings, so as not to upset him. Then they prayed together that their Dad and husband would go peacefully, when the Lord came to take him 'home'.

The next few days surely tested the strength of the family. What with the sleepless nights, the constant bedside vigils and keeping up with the work at the farm, it was a strain on all of them. Cindy's courage and strength kept everyone going, as they went through their day to day routine. William became the main concern now, so most of their time was spent with him. And a portion of that time was spent in the chapel, praying for William.

After a quick supper at the house, Cindy and the kids headed back to the hospital to visit with William. Samantha noticed her Dad's smile seemed awfully weak but she hugged him tight anyway and told him how much she loved him. Her Mother and brothers each did the same, then sat down in the chairs that the nurses had brought in for them. The doctor had already forewarned the family that it could be any time that this awful disease might take William from them. There was nothing more, that anyone could do. So, each moment spent with him was cherished by all of them.

As expected, William's time on earth was to be cut short by this dreadful disease. Thankfully, the family was with him when he breathed his last breath. Final 'good-byes' were said and hugs were given. It was so very hard to let go, even though they all knew that this day would come. William went to be with the 'Lord' peacefully, as the family had prayed for so diligently. The sorrow that each of them felt was so deep. Samantha was thankful that her Dad had not suffered in agony during his last days.

Cindy immediately began making funeral arrangements for the service, so as not to forget any details. Though it was the hardest thing that she had ever been through in her life, Cindy felt that William was at peace. And she was calmed by that thought alone.

Cindy's children continued to help out on the farm the next few days, so she could finalize the funeral arrangements. Cindy's friend, Linda, was a tremendous help with the luncheon preparations. This gave Cindy some time to go through photographs of William for the service.

Cindy had a hard time choosing just a few. She eventually decided on three pictures that she thought were the best. One picture was of William by himself, one with her and William in it and the third was of William and the children. Though none of this had been easy for her, Cindy felt an inner peace.

She would now be the 'soul provider' for her children. This brought a warm feeling to her heart because William had taught her many things about finances. Cindy had several savings bonds for her children that she and William had begun when they each were born. She knew that these would help each of them, whether they went off to college or started a new life on their own.

Samantha and the boys made sure that their clothes for the funeral service were pressed and ready for tomorrow. Cindy herself had chosen a favorite black dress that William himself had bought for her, on their anniversary. She hoped that everything was all set for the service. William deserved a wonderful celebration of his life here on earth and Cindy hoped that this would be a fitting tribute to her husband.

Friends and family gathered in the small Baptist Church, where the family had been regular attenders for many years. Cindy had asked for William's favorite hymn, 'Amazing Grace', to be played while people were taking their seats. This old hymn was a fitting one for William. There had been nothing that could have turned him away from his faith in God!

The service began promptly at eleven o'clock and of course, as everyone had expected, there was 'standing room' only in this small country Church. William had been well known and well-loved by many people. So, this was no surprise to Cindy to see the crowd of people gathered here in respect and love for her husband! There were so many friends that Cindy hadn't seen in years, at this service for William. Cindy thought that this was a wonderful tribute to a life-long friend and neighbor.

Pastor Mike began the service with a story about William. A story that William himself might have told, had he been given the opportunity. At one time, a few years back, their cows had gotten out. William had tried to steer the cattle back to the barnyard but the cows had a different idea. William was furious about the whole thing. He ran to the barn to call his neighbor, John, to help him. In his haste, he had fallen into the manure pile! This made William furious. But his family found it hilarious, and they had a hard time containing their laughter.

When the laughter subsided, Pastor Mike said, 'William was a helpful friend to his fellow man'. 'Many a time he had offered his help to his neighbors and friends'. 'When Tyler Smithson needed help with a new roof', 'William volunteered his services to him', the Pastor told the audience. In no time at all, the two men had shingled half of the roof and were ready for a break. Tyler's wife, Char, had made some iced tea for them.

In the process of getting down from the roof, William had caught his pants on a nail and had split them at the seam. Unknown to him, Tyler and Char had a good laugh over it! William had been a good sport through all of the ribbing and joking through the years. Many memories of William were brought back that day by several friends, who had known him for many years. The service was a wonderful tribute to William's life. Cindy thought it all very fitting for the man she had loved for twenty-five years!

Chapter nine

It had already been a month since William's passing. Cindy had done her best to keep things going on the farm. She had talked to Scott and Charles about selling the cattle. They had all agreed that it was a good idea, especially now that the boys were talking about moving out, on their own. First, they needed to find out the going rate for cattle, in order to get the best price for their cows.

Scott took a drive to the livestock sale on Saturday, to see what the cattle were selling for. He needed to be sure that they would get the best possible price for their beef cattle. It seemed they were going for a pretty good price and he thought his Mom would agree with him. He walked back to his pickup truck and headed back home to tell his Mother and brother the good news.

Scott wasn't paying attention to the posted signs and was driving over the speed limit. Before he knew it, he was being pulled over by a county sheriff. Scott's mind had been on his Dad's passing and several other things, so he was not paying attention to his speed.

The officer asked for proof of Insurance and I.D., which Scott searched for immediately. As he searched for the information, the officer saw something fall out of the glove box. He then asked Scott to step out of the truck, then, he asked him to stand with his hands on the roof of his truck. Scott was then told that he was under arrest for possession of marijuana.

Scott had forgotten that his friend, Paul had given him a small amount of 'weed', one evening after his Dad had passed away. Paul had thought that it might help Scott relax some. Unfortunately, Scott had forgotten about the illegal drug in his vehicle! He needed to call his Mother as soon as he was given the opportunity. This was so humiliating! Scott wasn't sure how he would tell his Mother, but he knew that he had no choice in the matter.

As he expected, Cindy was not happy about Scott's carelessness. But she was his only chance to get out of jail. And that would not happen until tomorrow morning. Scott would be spending the night in jail and would have plenty of time to think about what he had done. Just the same, Cindy knew that her eldest son was scared and ashamed. She hoped that his court date would yield a fair verdict for her son.

Since his Dad had passed away, Scott had been under a lot of pressure. Being the oldest had left him feeling responsible for his family and their well-being. Scott had taken the marijuana from his friend and put it into the glove box in his truck that evening. Now, he would pay for his it, literally!! Cindy had called her attorney and set up an appointment with him for a consultation. If only William was here, maybe this wouldn't have happened, Cindy thought to herself. She could only hope that Scott had learned a lesson from all of this. It just may be a very valuable lesson that he would carry with him for a long time.

Scott's court date was set for Tuesday, March 9th, at 10:00 A.M. Scott was very glad to get this whole thing over with and get on with his life. He hurried to get dressed in his suit and tie, his main objective was to make a good impression with the judge today. As Cindy drove to the county Courthouse, she prayed that the judge would be fair with her son. Scott had been a good citizen up until now, anyway!

Judge Wilkins would be presiding over the hearing that morning, which made Scott a little less nervous. He had heard that Mr. Wilkins was an understanding judge, so in turn, he hoped for some kind of good luck today. Just maybe, he would go easy on him, being this was his first offense and all! Scott sat down and waited for his Mother in the waiting area of the old Courthouse.

Cindy arrived at the courthouse a short while after Scott did. She found her son waiting for her patiently on a bench near the entrance to the historic courtroom. The nerves began to get to Scott once again, as they headed into the courtroom. It had been an uneasy morning for him and it was time to 'face the music'. They took their seats and waited for the judge to enter the room. All were asked to stand, as Judge Wilkins took his place at the front of the courtroom. Finally, Scott's trial would begin. As he was sworn in, Scott breathed a sigh of relief to know that this ordeal would be behind him soon!

Scott was given the opportunity to tell his side of the story, but he also had to 'rat' on his friend, Paul. He couldn't lie about what had happened that evening. That would only make matters worse! It turned out that Judge Wilkins had gone easy on Scott and had given him a sentence of ten hours of Community Service and a $100.00 fine. This suited Scott just fine. Cindy also was happy for the light sentence for her son.

Cindy and Scott left the Courthouse and headed over to get some lunch at the corner deli. Relieved to be out of there, Scott told his Mother about his fear of a stronger sentence from Judge Wilkins. 'Mom, I was terrified in there', Scott told her. 'I thought that he was going to 'throw the book at me today'! 'Well', Cindy began. 'You are pretty lucky, sir', she told him. They ordered their lunch and talked for a while before parting ways and heading back to their respective jobs.

The Weston's cattle were being sold to a gentleman just south of the county line. He was coming to pick them up on Friday, at 11:00 A.M. It would be strange not to have to worry about milking the cows. Scott chatted with his brother as they walked to the barn. It was time to corral the cows into the barn, in order to keep them dry for delivery on Friday. 'Do you think that Dad would have made the decision to sell the cows? Charles asked his older brother. 'I don't know', Scott answered. 'I guess it may have depended on his health at the time', Scott said. ' I hope that we're doing the right thing', Charles replied.

As the two brothers rounded the cattle up, Samantha and her Mom made supper. Samantha inquired of her Mother, 'Why did Scott smoke marijuana'? Cindy thought for a moment before answering her. 'Scott had been under some stress after your Dad passed away, and I think that maybe he made just made a bad choice that night'. Cindy hoped that she had answered Samantha's question for her. At this point, she wasn't sure that she herself knew why Scott had the marijuana. She had surely talked to each of them about drugs. But she wondered if they truly had listened!!

Cindy assured her daughter that Scott had learned a valuable lesson from all of this, and had vowed to never do it again. Samantha finished setting the table then began slicing the home-made bread that her Mom had made. All the while wondering, why would anyone want to abuse their body with drugs, anyway?

Samantha hadn't seen Tom since her Dad's funeral service, so she was surprised to see him show up at her doorstep on Saturday afternoon. He asked quietly, 'How are you and your family getting along?' 'We're getting by O.K.', Samantha answered. 'Mom sold the cows to lessen some of the burden on my brothers', she continued. 'Mom is also talking about selling some of the property or possibly leasing it to someone'. 'If your Mom needs help with anything, please let me know', Tom offered. 'Thank-you Tom', 'you've been so very kind to ask', Samantha stuttered.

Samantha had forgotten how easy it was to talk with him, she almost felt like Tom was a true friend to her and her family. She found herself pouring her heart out to him, about her Dad, and her brother's trouble with the Law. It was good to have someone to listen to her thoughts, after everything that had happened in her life, these past few months.

Tom politely excused himself to go to work at the pizza parlor in town. He reminded Samantha sweetly, that his offer to take her on a date still stood, as soon as she turned sixteen. She said 'good-bye' to her friend and wished him a good day at work. 'Thank you Samantha', he told her as he headed out the front door. Samantha hoped to herself that she would get the opportunity to go out with Tom. He was definitely a sweet guy and she sure wouldn't mind going on a date, if her Mother agreed. Samantha couldn't hide her smile as she walked into the kitchen. Cindy noticed the big grin on her daughter's face and knew exactly what she was thinking. 'So, what is Tom up to these days?' Cindy asked her daughter. 'Oh, he was going to work in town', Samantha told her. 'You really like him', 'don't you?' Cindy asked. 'Yes Mom, I do', Samantha told her as she grabbed her jacket.

Samantha headed outside to do her chores. She took note of how beautiful the day was and realized that summer really was just around the corner. But with a sudden sadness, Samantha realized that her Dad would not be around for her sixteenth birthday this year. She knew that he would still be there in spirit but it just wouldn't be the same!

Chapter ten

The time had come for Cindy to begin sorting through William's things but she wasn't sure where to begin. She chose to begin at William's dresser. This was where William had kept his favorite keepsakes in a cedar box. Cindy pulled the box down off the top of the dresser and sat down on the bed. When Cindy opened the cedar box, she found an envelope with her name on it. Inside the envelope was a letter from her late husband and a heart-shaped locket.

Cindy's heart pounded loudly as she opened the tiny locket. Inside was a picture of her and William on their wedding day. She thought to herself what a wonderful man that she had married. His thoughtfulness was immeasurable. As Cindy opened the letter, she felt a lump in her throat. It began with, 'My dearest Cindy, 'I know that you will find this long after I'm gone'. 'But just the same, I couldn't leave you without telling you how much I love you'. Tears streamed down Cindy's face as she continued reading.

Cindy read how William had never loved anyone as much as he had loved her. And he also wrote how he thanked God for her and his family, every day that he was on this earth. Cindy realized that there was no man that could ever take his place in her heart and she too had thanked God for him. She decided to wait until another day to begin the sorting. As she looked into the dresser mirror, Cindy thought how lucky she had been to have met and married William Weston!

Cindy hurried downstairs to tell her children about the letter and the locket. To her surprise, William had told them about his secret, and had made them promise not to tell their Mother! Samantha admired the locket for a moment before handing it back to her Mom. Noticing an engraving on the back, Samantha asked her Mother to read it. 'Forever, My One True

Love', these were the words on the back of it. Cindy was so overwhelmed, she began crying once again.

The family shared a group hug. At that moment, each one knew how very much that William would be missed! His spirit would live on forever in each of their hearts. It surely had not been easy losing a loved one, but the Weston family was determined to carry on, as William would have wanted them to. And so it would be as William wished!

Chores were now at a minimum, on account of the cattle being sold. So, life had been a little easier for the family at the farm. As of the spring of next year, a farmer would be leasing the acreage behind the barn. Cindy could now breathe a sigh of relief. Things were starting to fall into place for everyone, finally!! It had been a long time coming and Cindy hoped that it would all work out.

Samantha smiled at the thought of her Dad's little 'quips'. She remembered how he always had poked fun at the 'not so funny' days that came along. Sometimes it was easier to laugh at yourself than to be serious all the time. William had always tried to live his life in that manner. There really had not been any other way for him!

Spring had arrived and there seemed to be some freshness to the morning air as Samantha stepped outside to catch the school bus. It surely had been a long winter in Ohio. With the cold temperatures and the passing of Samantha's Dad behind them, it seemed to be time for a new beginning now. Samantha felt that her family would be alright, no matter what!

The Weston family had always had a strong faith in God. Their early days had been spent at Sunday school and church services. The children had been taught at an early age to trust in their Savior. This had helped them all through many a trying time in their lives.

After arriving at school, Samantha hurried to her classes. She saw some friends that were sitting alone and pulled a chair up next to them. 'How are you Samantha?' Julie asked. 'I'm doing alright, thank-you', Samantha answered. The small group of friends seemed to be together, in many of the same classes. This made it easy, in case someone forgot an assignment, or missed a day of school.

The day went by quickly. Before Samantha knew it, lunchtime had arrived! The rest of the day went by just as quick and Samantha thought she was in a time warp or something! Her classes seemed to fly by. It was so unusual for the school day to go by so fast! Oh well, she wasn't complaining, anyway. At least not today, she was in a fantastic mood and nothing was going to change that.

As the school day came to an end, Samantha walked to her locker to retrieve her homework. She was met by Tom and that beautiful smile. What a great way to end her school day! 'Would you like to come to my house for dinner tonight?' Tom asked her. Samantha responded with, 'I will ask my Mom and call you when I get home'. He patted her on the shoulder and said that he hoped he would see her later. Samantha grinned to herself as she gathered her things and went outside.

Samantha was ecstatic to hear her Mom say 'Yes', to her dinner invitation to Tom's house. She ran upstairs to pick out something to wear. She laid out several different outfits, before choosing one that looked just right! Samantha ran downstairs to show her Mom what she had picked out to wear to Tom's house. 'You look pretty, Samantha', her Mother told her. 'Scott will drop you off at Tom's house', 'And, I will pick you up, after dinner', Cindy told her. 'Thanks Mom', Samantha told her.

Samantha called out to her brother, to see if he was ready to go. Scott came running down the steps like a crazy man! 'Come on, let's go', he ordered. 'I've got a date with Lisa and I don't want to be late', he stammered. Samantha scolded her brother with, 'Slow it down mister'. 'You act like you are going to a fire or something'! They hurried out the door and jumped into his old truck. Tom didn't live far from Samantha, so they arrived there in a short amount of time. Samantha rang the doorbell and waited there. Tom answered the door and politely invited her inside. Samantha graciously thanked Tom's parents for inviting her. Dinner smelled delicious and was waiting for them on the dining room table when they all sat down. Mr. Halson asked that they all bow their heads, so he could give thanks for the meal.

Samantha was asked how her family was getting along, since her Dad's passing. 'They are doing well, considering the circumstances', Samantha replied. 'Thank you for asking', she finished. Mrs. Halson had made the most delicious lasagna. Samantha couldn't believe what a wonderful cook she was! And she made sure that she let her know about it. 'Mrs. Halson, this meal is wonderful', Samantha told her. 'Please, call me Katie', Tom's Mother told her. 'And thank you, Samantha'.

After the dinner dishes were done, Samantha sat with the Halson family while they visited and caught up on all the news. Samantha felt at ease with Tom's family. It was as if they had all known each other for a while. It had been a nice evening for everyone to sit and talk together. Samantha noticed the time and thanked Tom's parents for their hospitality. She knew that her Mom would be waiting for her outside and she didn't want to make her wait.

'Good-night everyone,' 'it was nice to meet you', Samantha said as Tom walked her to the door. He too thanked Samantha for coming for dinner, then, gave her a kiss on the cheek. Surprised, Samantha was at a loss for words for a moment! 'Thank-you for inviting me over for dinner, Tom', Samantha told him when she got her bearings. And then she gave him a hug in return. 'Good-night', each said to the other as Samantha walked out the front door.

Cindy was waiting, as Samantha expected, so she scurried to get into her Mother's mini-van. 'So, how did it go tonight', Cindy asked her daughter. "It went well, Mom', Samantha answered. 'Tom has a great family'. Samantha proceeded to tell her Mom about the meal that Katie had prepared. She also told of her collection of teacups that Katie had collected over the years. 'Mom, 'You would be amazed at the variety of tea cups that Tom's Mother has'!

Cindy decided that she might have quite a lot in common with Katie. Even though she hadn't met her yet, she felt as if she would get along just fine with her! Samantha couldn't wait to get home, so she could call Melissa and tell her about her evening at Tom's House. Melissa already knew that Samantha was 'sweet' on Tom, so it didn't surprise her at all that she had been invited to his home. 'Samantha, 'you are a lucky girl', Melissa told her. 'Tom is a nice boy and comes from a good family', she continued. Samantha replied with, 'I wish for you the same kind of friendship Melissa'. 'You deserve to be happy too'! Samantha told her best friend. The two talked for a few minutes before saying good-bye. Samantha put her pajamas on and brushed her teeth before crawling into her bed. She was happy that she had been invited to dinner at Tom's house. She fell asleep thinking about the evening's events, and of Tom's kiss!

Chapter eleven

To Samantha, it seemed that this spring had flown by. But she looked forward to July, when she would turn 'Sweet Sixteen'! Samantha had waited for this year to come and it was now a reality. A date with Tom was a possibility for her. As she gathered the eggs that afternoon, Samantha felt pretty happy with herself. It truly was turning out to be a good start to the year and she looked forward to the rest of it! Samantha felt that her family was going to make it. After all of the trials and tribulations they had been through, it was time for a new beginning.

The 'Good Lord' had always looked after the family. Even when things looked bleak, there was something positive that came out of such predicament. Some type of lesson was most often taught during their times of strife. And because of it, the family had become stronger, not only in their bond as a family but also in their faith. Samantha said a little prayer and went inside to help her Mom with supper.

It wouldn't be long before Samantha would take her driver's training classes. She was excited to learn to drive but at the same time, a little nervous. Cindy had just gotten a new mini-van which had all of the 'bells and whistles' that the new cars these days came with. Samantha was excited to drive it, as long as her Mother agreed to it.

Cindy had volunteered at the Church to help with the annual rummage sale on Saturday. Samantha tagged along with her to see if she help set up for the sale. Little did Samantha know, but Tom was also helping out at the Church that morning. As she went over to get her Mother a cup of coffee, in walked Tom and his Mother. What a surprise! 'Hey, 'how are you?'

Samantha asked. 'We are well', Tom's Mother said as she gave Samantha a hug. Samantha took her Mother the cup of coffee and asked her friends to join them.

Tom and Samantha each helped their Mothers set up the tables for the sale, then sat and talked for a while. Samantha told Tom about getting her learner's permit from driver's training class. Tom was a year older than her so he had been driving for about a year already. After a while, it was time to help out at the sale. People were starting to file into the dining area to look at the items for sale.

All in all, the sale went pretty fast. Customers came in and out, some making a purchase, others looking for something unique in their search. Samantha was in awe at the variety of collector's who searched for baseball cards and sports memorabilia. It had been a day of sales for the Missions fund at the Church. Nearly twelve hundred dollars had been raised for a good cause. And it was time to close up 'shop' for the day.

Cindy thanked Samantha for her help as they climbed into the van. Both were tired after a long day at the Church and were ready for a good hot supper. Cindy stopped at the corner grocery store on the way home to get some milk. Samantha waited in the van as her Mother went into the store. After a few minutes, Samantha noticed a scuffle going on in the parking lot. It seemed there was a ragged-looking man trying to steal a woman's purse! Samantha jumped out of the van to help the woman only to realize the woman was her Mother!

Samantha thought quickly and grabbing a shopping cart, began ramming it into the man. She repeatedly hit the man, hoping to get him away from her Mother. Another man saw the commotion and called the police. By the time the police arrived, Samantha had kicked the would-be mugger in the kneecap. This had kept him down until help had arrived. The policeman put handcuffs on the man and put him into the police cruiser's back seat, as Samantha tended to her Mother.

Cindy was just a little shaken up but no harm done. Thank goodness that Samantha had been paying attention. Samantha hugged her Mom tightly as the police car drove off with the criminal inside. 'Mom', 'I cannot let you go anywhere by yourself after this'! Samantha half begged her Mother. 'People are just too unpredictable'! She finished.

Samantha's summer vacation would begin in a couple of weeks which meant there would be a 'sweet sixteen' celebration in order. She had already signed up for her junior year classes and she had also completed her driver's training classes. Needless to say, Samantha was more than ready for this summer break! A few times, Samantha had driven with her Mother and thought that it was a 'piece of cake', although the parallel parking was not so easy for her.

Samantha finished her homework, then, called Melissa, to see how she and her family were getting along. Melissa told Samantha that her Mother was in the hospital because of her issues with her diabetes. 'They are trying to get her stable enough to come home', Melissa told Samantha. She replied to her friend with, 'I'm sorry, Melissa'. 'I hope she'll be able to come home soon'. 'Thank-you, Samantha'. "I better say 'good-bye for now'. It was late and time for bed, so the girls said 'good-night'.

Samantha turned in for the night after she said her nightly prayers. The dream of her Wedding Day again became part of her sleep time that evening. But still, each time she dreamed it, Samantha could not see her Groom's face. Sometimes, she woke up feeling very frustrated about her dream. What could it mean? Samantha wondered, as she got ready for school the next day.

Cindy's Court date to contend with the man that had tried to mug her had arrived. She would need to be at the courthouse at 3:00 P.M. this afternoon. Cindy was not looking forward to seeing the creepy little man again. She set aside her angst and drove to the courthouse. Scott had been charged for the felony that he had committed at the same courthouse, just a couple of months ago.

Cindy parked her car and put a few coins into the parking meter. Then she made her way into the courthouse. It was to be a closed hearing today, so there were very few people sitting in the courtroom. Cindy's friend, Linda had showed up for moral support. She was sitting with Samantha, who of course had been a key witness to the whole scenario.

The proceedings didn't take long as Cindy had hoped for. She breathed a sigh of relief as the judge handed down the 'would-be' thief's sentence. A month in jail and substantial court fees were given to the man who thought he should have Cindy's purse that day. What a relief! Hopefully, he had learned his lesson, Cindy thought to herself. The three women exited the courthouse together, talking about the little man and his beady eyes. Anyway, it was over! They all were thankful that he would be serving time for his crime.

Samantha was thankful that she had been there that day for her Mother's sake. Who knows what might have happened had she not been there? The situation could have escalated had Cindy been alone that day. Samantha shuddered at the thought! Her Mother's 'guardian angel' had been looking out for her that day. That was for sure!

Samantha and Cindy got home that afternoon, to find Charles lying on the sofa, in dire pain, claiming that he just did not feel well. Charles had always been a quiet person. Almost an introvert at times, he still managed to be well-liked by his many friends. His Mother knew that this was something serious so she hurried to get her son to the van. 'Scott, please pack a bag for your brother', Cindy called out to Scott. 'He's going to the hospital, now', she said.

No time was wasted getting to the hospital. After they arrived, Charles was admitted with appendicitis. Emergency surgery was done on Samantha's brother as they waited in the lobby of the hospital. Charles had just been hired at the feed mill in town, so Samantha wondered how long her brother would need to recover. Samantha prayed for her brother's fast recovery as she waited for her Mother to return from the nurse's station.

Charles' stay at the hospital was short, which meant that he could come home on Saturday. Cindy and Samantha re-arranged the living room so Charles could stay on the sofa for a while until he recovered. Samantha agreed to help with chores while her brother was on the mend. She agreed to help feed the pigs, but wasn't happy about walking through the smelly barn! But for her brother, she would do it. It would only be for a few days until Charles felt better. Samantha supposed she could set aside her 'smelly barn' issues until her sibling was feeling better. It was what she needed to do!

Cindy cooked supper for everyone, but was careful to include foods that Charles could eat also. His doctor had ordered that Charles eat only soft food for a few days. At least until his stomach was up to it, anyway. The family sat and enjoyed the meal together. Samantha and Cindy sat in the living room with Charles so he wouldn't have to eat alone. The meal was topped off with some of Cindy's home-made butterscotch pudding. Delicious!

With his family's loving care, Charles would be back to his old self in no time. He wasn't used to so much pampering! But somehow, he would get himself accustomed to it. During his recovery, Charles had often thought of his Dad. He remembered the days when William had taken Charles and his brother fishing at the creek on their property. How William had taught the two of them to bait their hooks, and, how to cast their lines, and the bond that the three of them had formed those many years ago. Charles missed his Dad dearly but knew that somehow, he was still with him!

As expected, Charles was back to his old self in no time! Samantha was happy not to have to do the pig chores anymore. She had smelled enough of those pigs to last a lifetime and she was glad to have Charles look after them again! Her brother laughed at her when she told him her woes about pig chores. 'It's not funny', Samantha told Charles. 'I hate smelling like a pig', she muttered, as she went upstairs to take a bath.

It would be only a matter of days before Samantha's birthday. She lay in bed and thought about her Dad and wished that he could be here for her special day. The empty place in her heart ached for her Dad's warm smile and his sunny disposition. Samantha fell asleep thinking of her beloved Dad. Although she knew that her memories of him would never fade, she felt a sadness that haunted her daily life without him.

Cindy had bought Samantha a beautiful pair of diamond stud earrings for her birthday, along with a very special 'surprise'.

Although Cindy was proud of all of her children, she was especially proud of Samantha. She had shown a level of responsibility that most young people didn't have at her age. So, Cindy wanted to make this birthday a very special one for Samantha.

As she sat down to watch the evening news, Cindy listened in astonishment, as the newscaster told of several break-ins in the area. One of which wasn't far from her office! She heard a familiar name as she sat and watched the broadcast. An attorney that she had known for many years had fallen victim to the crimes at his place of business. Cindy thought to herself, 'What if the thieves had stolen personal information or confidential files of clients'? 'Would they begin causing trouble for those innocent victims'? She wondered. The hair on the back of her neck stood up as she wondered if her employer's office would be next!!

Since William had passed on, Cindy had found that she now worried more about little things more and more. She knew that she shouldn't worry about such trivial stuff, but sometimes, she couldn't help herself. She turned off the television and finished the supper dishes. When she was finished, she sat down with her Bible and read a few chapters before getting ready for bed.

As Cindy sat and read, Samantha came downstairs and sat down with her Mother. Hoping to spend some Mother-daughter time, Samantha leaned against her Mother's shoulder. 'Mom, do you miss Dad like I do'? Samantha asked quietly. Cindy thought for a moment before responding. 'I do miss your Dad, Samantha', 'but in a different way than you do", Cindy continued. 'We were friends for many years and when you lose your best friend, it takes some getting used to', Cindy said sadly.

Chapter twelve

Samantha was on 'Cloud Nine', as she awoke on the morning of her 'Sweet Sixteen' birthday. Not only was she about to get her driver's license, she was old enough to go on a date too! Cindy had already had the infamous, 'birds and bees' talk with Samantha and she had vowed to be responsible in her relationships with any boys. As Samantha got ready for the day, she wondered what was in store for her birthday today. No matter what, it was going to be the best day ever! At least in Samantha's world, it would be.

Cindy finished decorating Samantha's birthday cake then she sat down for a moment to reminisce about Samantha's younger days. Cindy remembered the day that her daughter had started kindergarten. Samantha stood at her desk, holding her lunchbox, waving at her Mom. "It's O.K. Mommy', 'You can leave now', Samantha had told her. With tears in her eyes, Cindy waved 'good-bye' and went outside to her car. It had been so hard to leave Samantha there at the school that morning!

Cindy smiled at the memory and was thankful to have such a wonderful daughter. Later that afternoon, everyone enjoyed home-made sloppy Joes and potato salad, in honor of Samantha's birthday. The delicious chocolate cake was gone in no time. Almost everyone had asked for a second helping that day. No matter, a good time was had by all of the guests that gathered in celebration that afternoon. Samantha was beaming from ear to ear just thinking about getting her driver's license, on Monday. Cindy had asked for some time off work, in order to take Samantha to the Secretary of State's office on Monday. Cindy had a big surprise for Samantha but it would have to wait until Monday afternoon!

After cleaning up the party mess, Samantha and Cindy sat down for a moment. Samantha thanked her Mother for the wonderful party and the great food too. 'Anything for you, Samantha', Cindy replied. 'You're 'the best', Mom', Samantha said to her Mother. Samantha hugged her Mother and told her how much she appreciated all that she did. The smile on Cindy's face told Samantha that she too was appreciative of her daughter.

According to Samantha, this weekend wasn't going by quickly enough! She was consumed by the thought of getting her very own driver's license and nothing else really mattered at this point. Samantha was jolted back to reality by her brother, Scott, yelling at her to get her chores done before the chickens starved to death! She simply yelled back at him and told him that the chickens weren't going to starve to death. 'Geez', 'Could you settle it down a bit? Samantha asked him, as she went outside to feed the chickens.

Samantha waited patiently for her Mother to get home. They were planning to attend the Vacation Bible School program at the Church that night. The children had been practicing their songs for a couple of weeks and were ready to show off what they had learned while at Bible School that summer. As Samantha waited, Cindy pulled into the driveway. Samantha ran out to greet her mother exclaiming, 'I thought you would never get home'!

Cindy hurried to change her clothes. Samantha met her at the bottom of the stairway. Cindy grabbed the cookies off the counter and off they went! In a hurry, Cindy drove to the Church instead of Samantha that evening. Neither wanted to miss the kids program, so they scurried to their seats with just minutes to spare!

The children had spent many hours rehearsing their songs and it had obviously paid off. Their voices were 'angelic'! The voice from Julie Hanes, a talented young girl who practiced weekly with her vocal coach, was fabulous. There was no doubt that these young children were destined to be great!! The applause was deafening, as the audience stood up and congratulated the group. The choir director, Susie Mason, also was cheered for her faithful service to the children's choir.

Finally, the pastor walked to the podium. He congratulated the children on their performances then invited the congregation to join the children for some refreshments. As Cindy and Samantha made their way to the dining room, they ran into Georgia Woods, a longtime friend of the family. Georgia had lost her husband to a heart attack five years before. She herself knew what Cindy was going through since William's passing. They all chatted for a while before sitting down with some refreshments along with the other guests.

Many of the youth performers stopped by the table to say their 'hellos' before enjoying their own treats that evening. Samantha was not surprised that there was so much talent in the Church. Some of the children came by it naturally. Others took lessons from local instructors to learn to perform in front of a crowd of people. Nonetheless, these were some very talented young members of the Church!

As many people began leaving, Samantha asked her Mother if they could leave also. 'I'm tired too', Cindy told Samantha. The two gathered their purses and headed outside to the parking lot. To their surprise, there had been a small 'fender bender'. Someone had backed into Jason Smith's car while they had been inside the Church. The damage was minimal, so there wasn't much to get excited about, at least not right now, anyway!

Cindy drew a hot bath when she arrived home and relaxed for a few moments before turning in for the night. She often thought of her loving husband and wished that she could hold him in her arms again. Although she knew that nobody would ever take William's place in her heart, Cindy ached for someone to talk to and laugh with again. Sleep came quickly and her dreams consisted of memories of her life with a wonderful loving husband, whom she never would forget!

Samantha waited patiently for her Mother to arrive home so that she could go and get her driver's license. She had waited for what seemed like forever for this day. A few more minutes wasn't going to make a big difference, so she sat and waited a while longer for her Mother. Cindy eventually drove up the long drive to their house and Samantha jumped into the car. 'So, is my youngest ready to get her license?' Cindy asked. A smile was all that Samantha could muster at this point.

Not much was said on the way to town. Samantha wanted this so badly that she couldn't think about anything else! Her nerves were getting the best of her and it showed on her face. Her Mother tried to calm her but she knew that Samantha would need to just relax and breathe before taking her test at the licensing office. Cindy was sure that her daughter would pass and be a licensed driver before too long now.

Samantha was given her copy of the written portion of the test, so she sat down to begin. Before too long, she had finished and was standing at the desk once again. As she quietly waited for the lady to give her the news, Cindy winked at her and gave Samantha a big smile. She had always had a way to calm Samantha. It had worked since she had been a newborn in her arms. And apparently, it still worked like a charm! Samantha had passed with 'flying colors', according to the nice lady behind the desk. Beaming, Samantha was told to stand on the 'x' in front of the desk. 'Smile', the woman told her as she snapped a picture of the brand new driver. Samantha just about jumped for joy but decided she shouldn't in case it might bother someone that might be taking their test. She had achieved what she had come here for so it was time to leave!

When they got outside, Cindy reminded Samantha that she had a surprise for her. 'Are you ready to go see your surprise?' Cindy asked her. 'I can't wait, Mom! Samantha replied excitedly. 'Let's go then', Cindy said as she drove off to their next destination. The butterflies in Samantha's stomach seemed to be playing 'tag' as the two drove towards the 'surprise'. A familiar neighborhood came into view. They were going to Grandma Berta's house!

As they pulled into the driveway, Samantha jumped out of the van and ran to the front door of her grandmother's house. Grandma was waiting for them inside. 'Hi, Grandma', Samantha said as she hugged her grandmother. Cindy followed Samantha into the house and hugged her Mother also. 'How is everyone?' Berta asked as they sat down to visit. 'We're all good Mom', Cindy replied. Samantha sat and fidgeted while the two other women talked about the latest news. Samantha's curiosity was just about to get the best of her when her Mother asked if she was ready for her 'Surprise'. 'Mom, 'the suspense is killing me!' Cindy answered her with, 'Well, let's go then'. Cindy walked through the kitchen, then, asked Samantha to close her eyes until she said to open them. Samantha closed her eyes tight as her Mother and Grandmother led the way out to the garage.

Cindy placed Samantha in front of the 'surprise' then asked her to open her eyes. When Samantha opened her eyes, she let out a shriek of delight that may have curdled milk, had it been any louder! There in front of her was a shiny new car wrapped in a giant, red bow. 'Is this for me?' Samantha asked. 'Yes, 'It's for you', Cindy replied. 'Well, what do you think?' Cindy asked. Samantha responded by giving her Mom one of the biggest hugs that she had ever been given!

Samantha ran around the car to get into the driver's seat. As she sat down, she asked her Mother if they could go for a drive. 'Sure, let's all go'. Cindy said. 'Mom, this is the best gift'! 'You're the best Mom ever', Samantha exclaimed as she started the engine of her new ride. This had to be the most fabulous gift that there had ever been, at least in Samantha's eyes! Her new red car had to be the best around this whole town and she couldn't wait to show it off!

They all climbed out of Samantha's car when they arrived at the ice cream parlor. It was a day of celebration and a root beer float was first on Samantha's mind. Cindy and Berta followed Samantha's lead and each ordered a root beer float also. They all sat down to enjoy their treat and talked about Samantha's new car. It was a beautiful day indeed and it would not soon be forgotten!

Samantha was hardly able to contain her excitement as she told her friends one by one about her new car! Melissa was very happy for Samantha but seemed to be down tonight. Samantha got her to admit that she and Joshua had quit seeing each other. 'I'm sorry, Melissa', Samantha told her friend. 'I'm trying to stay busy helping out at home', 'but it's hard to keep my mind off of Joshua', Melissa told her. It would take some time to get over Joshua but Melissa was a strong girl and was determined to go on with her life.

The two finished their conversation and said 'good-night'. Samantha loved her friend, Melissa. She wished they could see each other more often but the miles between them kept them apart. Samantha prayed for Melissa to meet some new friends in Oregon. She knew that Melissa needed someone to keep her mind busy, while her broken heart was on the mend. Samantha lay awake for a short while longer before falling asleep. It had been a day that was full of new beginnings and a brand new car! And Samantha was one of the luckiest girls in the world!

Chapter thirteen

A couple of months had passed since Samantha had gotten her car. She loved the fact that she had her own 'wheels' now. All of Samantha's friends thought that she was one of the luckiest girls to have a car of her very own!

Soon, school would be starting. Samantha would be a junior at her high school this year. She wondered how time had flown by so quickly for her. Where had it gone to? Samantha remembered her days in elementary school and smiled at how time dragged by back then. At least it seemed to go by real slow in those days. You waited forever for Christmas to arrive, your birthday, even Halloween took sweet time arriving!! And now, Samantha hardly seemed to have enough hours in a day anymore.

Samantha and Cindy were planning a school shopping trip with Linda and Susie. Samantha had still not gotten over the fact that she had seen Susie smoking cigarettes, but knew that Linda had talked to Susie about the 'habit' she had picked up.

That evening, after supper, Samantha went outside to enjoy the beautiful summer evening with her Mother. As they sat on the porch swing, they talked of memories of William. Each of them missed him dearly and neither could ever forget his presence in their lives. He had left a mark on everyone with his kind, loving ways. William would not soon be forgotten! He would remain a chapter in their lives that they would hold within their hearts forever.

Saturday morning arrived and the women were ready to take on a shopping trip. They all were hoping to find some bargains that day. Because she would be starting a new year at High School this fall, fashion was all the rage to Samantha. She wanted to look her best and intended to do just that!

Once arriving at the mall, the four women hit the shoe stores first thing. Susie had been 'eyeing' a certain pair of black boots. Samantha said they were 'great' and told Susie that she should try them on. 'Mom, these boots are fabulous', Susie told her Mother. Linda replied, 'Well then, we better get them for you'. Samantha eventually found a pair of shoes for herself also.

After shopping all morning, the two girls had bought some clothes to start the new school year with. Shopping had tired everyone out, so they stopped to rest at a soda shop for a moment. Refreshed again, the four friends headed for the parking lot with their bags. It had been a long day and it was time to go home and relax!

Linda invited Cindy and Samantha inside for some iced tea but they asked for a 'rain check' for another day. 'Good-bye then', Linda told them as she went inside the house. Then, as Cindy backed out of Linda's driveway, the unthinkable happened!

A young driver not paying attention, had broad-sided their van. Cindy was frantic when she realized that Samantha had been injured. She called out to her daughter but got no response from her. Cindy jumped out of the van and ran to the other side to try to get to Samantha. She couldn't get the door open and called out for help. Linda had seen what had happened and had already called the ambulance. Samantha was bleeding profusely from her head and Cindy tried her best to contain her fear for her daughter's life!

Linda tried to keep Cindy calm but was having a hard time herself remaining quiet about the situation. 'The ambulance will be here any minute' was all that Linda managed to say to her friend. Her nerves were getting the best of her as she waited helplessly for the paramedics to arrive.

As they heard the sirens approaching, the women stood and embraced one another and prayed for Samantha. As they hugged, Linda noticed that Cindy had a nasty bruise on her arm. 'You might want the paramedics to look at that', Linda told her. 'No, I'm fine', Cindy replied. 'Samantha is the one who needs their attention right now'!

As the paramedics removed Samantha from the wrecked van, Cindy cried out to her saying, "I'm sorry honey', 'Mom's going stay right with you', she sobbed to her. As they put Samantha into the ambulance, Cindy climbed into the back with her. She grabbed hold of Samantha's hand and prayed once more for her beloved daughter. When her vitals were stable, the paramedic named Paul spoke with Cindy about Samantha's injuries. It was all so frightening to be sitting there with her daughter hooked up to "IV' tubes and monitors! It was almost too much to bear all at once. Cindy sobbed again and asked Paul if Samantha would be 'O.K'. He answered her with, "It's hard to say right now, Ma'am', but as soon as we get her to the emergency room, they'll be able to better check her injuries'.

Cindy half smiled and thanked the man while hoping that Samantha would be alright. So many thoughts were running through her mind right now that nothing made any sense at this point. All she could hope for was that Samantha would pull through this horrible accident!

Finally, they arrived at the hospital. Samantha was whisked inside and taken immediately into a private room. Several doctors hovered around her as they tried to determine the extent of her injuries. Cindy quietly waited outside of Samantha's room as Linda tried her best to comfort her friend. It was all so unreal! Just months ago, Cindy had sat here while William had gone through his ordeal with cancer.

The doctor had finally come out to tell Cindy about Samantha's injuries. She had suffered head and neck trauma and was in a coma. Severe bleeding on her brain had been found along with her other injuries. It would be a long hard road for Samantha. Cindy sat and waited for the opportunity to see Samantha. It would be a while before they would get her vital signs stable enough for her to have any visitors. Cindy could not believe that she was here now because of someone else's carelessness! It was so maddening. Cindy tried to calm herself down but the thought of Samantha lying there helpless, was taking her nerves to the breaking point!

All that Cindy could do was to pray. And pray she did, fervently, over and over again. This felt like a horrible dream and she just wanted it to be over with! Linda arrived with a couple of cups of coffee for the two of them. Cindy looked up at Linda and asked, "why do bad things happen to my family?' Linda could not come up with any reason to give her friend. 'I can't answer that. Cindy', was all she said.

Cindy had a hard time leaving Samantha's side at the hospital but Linda made sure that she went home to rest now and then. Most nights, Cindy would sleep in the waiting room. Her sleep had been restless because the accident kept re-playing in her mind over and over again. Could she have avoided the situation all together? Cindy wondered to herself. She tried not to beat herself up over it but the guilt weighed heavy on her mind every day.

By the next morning, Cindy was real worried about Samantha, so she called Pastor Mike to ask if he would come to the hospital. Pastor Mike was happy to stop in and pray over Samantha's bed as he had been asked to. The sight of Samantha lying there was enough to make tears well up in his eyes! He had known the family for many years and had watched all of the kids grow up before him.

Cindy stood quietly near Samantha's bed as the Pastor said a prayer for her speedy recovery. As Pastor Mike left, Cindy thanked him for coming here for her daughter and then she bid him 'good-bye'. She sat quietly for a while longer before leaving to go home for a short while. Scott and Charles were arriving at the hospital as Cindy was leaving. She hugged both her sons and told them there had been no change in Samantha's condition, at least at this point.

Cindy drove Linda's car home that morning. She hadn't been home in two days and it was strange not to have her own van to drive. When she arrived home, Cindy took a quick shower, then, threw some things into an overnight bag for herself. Just in case she stayed at the hospital, she wanted to have her toothbrush and her comb at least. Samantha had been in a coma for two days now and it seemed there weren't any changes as of yet. The 'Good Lord' only knew what the future held for Samantha!

Scott and Charles took their turns sitting with their sister. Both young men felt crushed by this accident but still prayed for Samantha's recovery just the same! For two brothers that didn't show their emotions, they sure showed their love for their sister on those days spent in her hospital room. It was the least that either of them could do for their baby sister!

While Cindy was at home recharging, Tom called to ask about Samantha's condition. They agreed to meet back at the hospital in about an hour before they finished their conversation. Cindy had just realized how Tom felt about Samantha. This fine young man was genuinely concerned about her daughter and this brought a smile to Cindy's face.

As he had promised, Tom was waiting for Cindy in the waiting room at the hospital when she arrived. Cindy smiled and thanked him for coming in then she asked Tom if he would like to see Samantha. 'Yes, I'd like to see her now', if I could', Tom told Cindy. When Tom walked into Samantha's room, his heart sank to see his friend, all bruised and battered! He pulled a chair up next to her bed and took hold of her small hand.

A tear rolled down his cheek as his emotions got the best of him. Tom had kept his feelings for Samantha under cover. He was afraid that she may not feel the same way about him and didn't want to upset her. The sadness for Samantha took over him and the tears flowed as he sat in silence by himself. A quiet man who kept his feelings to himself, he could not contain them anymore! His love for Samantha had to be told even if it meant embarrassing himself in front of her family. Tom needed to let someone know about this before it was too late! He squeezed Samantha's hand tighter as he prayed for his friend and for the courage to tell of his feelings for her.

Tom spoke softly to Samantha as she lay there, fighting for her young life. He spoke of his love for her even though she may not hear his words. He confessed to her how he had felt since grade school and his feelings had only grown stronger for her over the years! Tom's disbelief that this had happened to his friend was unfathomable. She was so innocent and young! Only by the grace of God, would Samantha pull through this horrible ordeal!

The days and nights that had been spent at the hospital seemed a blur to Cindy. It had been two months since the accident and still no change in Samantha's condition. Dr. Hin had told Cindy that Samantha had her age on her side, and this was a sign that she would possibly come through this ordeal. It was all a matter of time and the waiting was the worst part for all of them!

Cindy thanked Dr. Hin for his words of encouragement. She sat down and watched Samantha as she lay in her small bed. Cindy held tight to her daughter's hand as she herself drifted off to sleep. It had been an exhausting few weeks and it was going to take a small miracle to bring Samantha back to her usual old self.

October had arrived suddenly and the leaves had already begun to change their colors once again. Cindy stepped outside to take in the fall splendor at the farm, before heading back to the hospital. It was these small things that helped Cindy keep her wits about her during Samantha's stay at the hospital. The beauty of nature had always had a calming effect on Cindy and this day was no exception!

When Cindy arrived back at the hospital that morning, she was greeted by a nurse at the front desk. It seemed there was some paperwork to sign before billing out to the Insurance Company. After signing the requested forms, Cindy went to Samantha's room with the flowers she had brought for the window ledge. As Cindy walked into the small room, she felt as if a weight had been lifted off her shoulders.

She settled in next to Samantha's bed and began reading out loud to her daughter. Cindy had read a couple of chapters to her, when something caught her eye. It seemed that Samantha was moving her fingers as if to say that she was listening!! Cindy jumped up and ran to the hallway and called to one of the nurses on duty. 'She moved', Cindy told the nurse. 'She moved her fingers!' she exclaimed to her. Cindy's heart was beating so fast that she thought she might just pass out. The nurse asked her to sit for a moment while she checked Samantha's vital signs. When the nurse was finished, Cindy leaned over her daughter and kissed her gently on the forehead. 'I love you', she whispered softly to Samantha as she held her hand once again. This was a very good sign that Samantha was coming back to them. Their prayers were beginning to be answered and Cindy was beside herself with happiness that morning!

As Dr. Hin talked with the nurses, Cindy thought that her heart might just beat right out of her chest! 'I believe that there is a good chance that your daughter may be waking up from her coma, Mrs. Weston', Dr. Hin told Cindy with a smile. 'We will need to run a few tests to verify my opinion, but I'm almost positive that this is a good sign'.

'Somebody will let you know as soon as we have some results', the good doctor told Cindy. She stepped out into the hallway as the team prepared to begin tests on Samantha. After saying a prayer of thanks, Cindy walked to the waiting room and poured herself a cup of coffee. She sat down to call her Mother with the news. Berta was very happy for Cindy and asked her to give Samantha her love for her.

For what seemed like hours, Cindy waited there for some news of Samantha's recovery. As she waited, Tom arrived to see how his friend was doing. Cindy was glad to see a familiar face again on this day of happiness for her beloved daughter. She was glad to tell Tom of the good news and he was thankful for his friend of many years. Tom gave Cindy a hug and told her how happy he was that Samantha may be 'out of the woods'. He kept his feelings quiet once again as he wanted to wait for just the right time to tell Samantha's family of his love.

All in good time, Tom told himself, all in good time. He walked with Cindy to the hallway outside of Samantha's room. They waited together for the doctor to come and give them the test results. Finally, a nurse came to them and asked them to wait in Samantha's room for the doctor. When Dr. Hin arrived, he told them that some of the results would not be available for a couple of days but as far as they could tell, there was some improvement in Samantha's condition.

Tom sat quietly and debated how he would tell Samantha of his love for her. He did not want to embarrass her or make her feel uncomfortable, so he decided it would need to be a very sweet display of his affection. Nothing was too good for his sweet little Samantha! And Tom intended it all to be just that!

Chapter fourteen

Cindy had fallen into her bed exhausted the night before, but had awoken with a sense of well-being the next morning. She hurried downstairs to make herself a pot of coffee and start the day. Linda called while she was drinking her coffee so Cindy proceeded to tell her about Samantha's improvement. Linda was glad to hear the good news about her young friend.

Cindy drove to the hospital once again and on her way, she thought about William's battle with cancer. He had put up a good fight even though he knew that there was a chance that he may not beat it. Cindy had a sense that Samantha might have her Dad's 'fight' in her and hoped that she was right about her gut feeling. If this were the case, Samantha had a good chance of pulling through this!

Cindy was curious to find out the rest of the test results on Samantha, so she asked for Dr. Hin when she arrived at the front desk of the hospital. The doctor would not come in until ten A.M., so Cindy waited in Samantha's room until he arrived. Samantha looked so small and meek laying there in that bed that Cindy couldn't help but think about when she was younger and needed her tonsils taken out.

Samantha had been eight years old when she started complaining about a sore throat. The family pediatrician had examined Samantha and determined that her tonsils and adenoids would need to be removed immediately! Needless to say, Samantha was not a 'happy camper'. But she had healed and was feeling better in no time after her surgery. Cindy smiled down at her beautiful daughter lying there and thanked God for her. She had brought something special to Cindy's life and she was grateful for her company.

Cindy stepped outside of Samantha's room for a moment to get some air. She met Tom coming down the hallway. 'Hello Cindy, 'how is our patient today?' Tom asked her. Cindy told him that they were still waiting for some test results but there had been some improvement from Samantha. Tom smiled and gave Cindy a hug. 'I have faith that God will heal our little Samantha', he half whispered to Cindy. 'You are a good friend to Samantha, Tom'. 'Thank you' she finished.

It was Tom's pleasure that he could be a friend to Samantha. Cindy had no idea how he felt about her daughter and it probably would be a while longer before his true feelings would be revealed. He thought to himself, what if Samantha wasn't interested in him? What on earth would he do? His heart could not withstand the crushing blow if that were to be the case!

It seemed that Tom and Cindy had waited for hours for the doctor to come and talk with them. When Dr. Hin arrived, the news was promising, as they both had hoped for! Samantha had shown many signs of improvement in the past few days which meant she very well may be on the road to recovery. Tom's heart skipped a beat at the news of Samantha's health. He knew that his friend was coming back to them. They both thanked God silently as they approached Samantha's room once again. Without all of the prayers and kind words, Samantha may not have come through this. Prayers really were being answered and Cindy couldn't be more ecstatic!

'Some of the hard times that we go through are a test of our faith', Cindy told Tom as they entered Samantha's room. Tom agreed that these things only made us stronger and ready to take on the next challenge in our lives. 'Loving friends and family sure don't hurt either', Tom replied with a grin. Tom sat with Cindy until it was time for him to leave for work. The two had talked for a short while that morning, both enjoying the other's company.

The terrible ordeal that Samantha had been through, meant that she would need a lot of time to heal from her injuries. Melissa had called the house since the accident and Cindy had been the one to tell her about Samantha's injuries. Melissa was surprised to hear of her friend's accident. 'Is there anything that I can do?' Melissa had asked Cindy that evening. 'No, Melissa, we're just waiting for time to heal Samantha's injuries'. 'It will be a long time before she is as good as new again', Cindy continued. 'Thank you for asking, Melissa', Cindy told Samantha's friend. Cindy could hear the concern in Melissa's voice and felt sorry that she couldn't be here in Ohio with her.

Tom whispered to Samantha 'good-night', before leaving her side that evening. He had spent the whole day with her. Cindy wasn't surprised at the time that Tom had spent with Samantha. His devotion to his friend was really very sweet!

Tom Halson was born on December 15, 1964 at Swanson Memorial Hospital. His parents, Dennis and Katie, were very happy to greet their new son. Katie had said that Tom was perfect! Ten little fingers and ten little toes, he had been born prematurely but had been healthy otherwise. Tom's parents had raised him to be an honest and forthright citizen. And his upbringing had paid off to his advantage!

Tom couldn't wait for Samantha to start recovering. He intended to get to know her better so they could begin spending more time together. As he himself crawled into his own bed that night, he prayed not only for his family and friends, but made a special prayer request for Samantha. A prayer for her to awaken from her deep and troubled sleep! Then he fell asleep hoping that his simple prayers would be answered.

It had been a very long few months that Samantha had been in a coma. Cindy breathed a sigh of relief as she waited for her daughter to come back to her. Cindy's hope for her youngest child to speak to her again was maddening. It was difficult to watch her lying there so helpless and frail. Many more days would pass before Samantha would awaken completely from her long sleep. Cindy felt comforted by the thought that Samantha's condition had improved slowly over the last few months. Even though she had been in a coma, there had been some healing while she had been out.

When the day arrived that Samantha had come out of her deep sleep, she had been confused and disoriented. The nurses reassured her that she was alright and that she had been in an accident. 'Where is my Mom?' She had asked immediately. 'She has been here every day', the young nurse told Samantha. It had been very hard at first for Samantha to focus her eyes when she woke up. The headaches that she dealt with every day were excruciating! Cindy tried to sooth Samantha but the pain sometimes was too much for her to bear.

Cindy allowed Samantha to rest most of the time while she was in her room. She told her of Tom's visits while she was in her coma. Samantha tried to put forth a smile when her Mother told her about all of the friends and family that had visited her. The prayers had been immeasurable and the support was amazing! Samantha couldn't believe the love that she had been given from everyone. It was great to be so loved and cared for during such a difficult situation.

'It is so good to hear your voice', Cindy told Samantha as they visited that sunny afternoon. 'I have missed you so much, Samantha'. 'I'm sorry Mom', Samantha replied. The women hugged and Cindy again kissed her daughter's forehead. 'You are so lucky, Samantha'. 'Someone was looking out for you and we both know who that is'. They smiled to think that the road to Samantha's recovery was here. Although there was no doubt that it would be a long and winding road!

Dr. Hin would not release Samantha until she could walk on her own. Physical therapy would take weeks but determined Samantha would not give up! She intended to get better, no matter how hard she had to work. Her well-being depended on it! Samantha had taken a few steps on her own but needed to be able to walk completely on her own free will. If she could pull it off, Dr. Hin would let her go home next Tuesday.

Tom had offered to tutor Samantha on some of her studies at school. She would not be allowed to go back to school for another couple of weeks. She kindly thanked Tom for his offer. 'I can come over on Wednesday if you would like' Tom told her as he left her hospital room. 'Great', Samantha told him with a smile. She felt so lucky to have such a good friend in Tom. She truly was blessed to have so many people that were happy to rally around her in her time of need.

Tom wasn't quite ready to confess his feelings to Samantha. He needed more time to get his nerve up. The timing had to be perfect in the situation with Samantha. 'Lord, please help me to have the strength to tell Samantha of my feelings for her', Tom prayed as he drove home that evening. He hoped that Samantha would feel the same way about him. He decided not to worry too much about it because it didn't pay to get bent out of shape over something like this.

Before bringing Samantha home, Cindy needed to arrange the house to accommodate Samantha's frail condition. The sofa was going to be a makeshift bed for Samantha while she was on the mend. Samantha's movements were slow at the moment, but Dr. Hin promised her that she soon would be back to her normal activities. That is, as long as she went to her physical therapy appointments when she was supposed to!

When Samantha arrived back home, she felt as if she had been away from home forever but it had really only been a few months that she had been gone. She took a deep breath as she walked into the house. Cindy had made roast beef for supper and Samantha was starving! The smell of real food was fantastic! Samantha could not wait to dig in to her Mom's good cooking again. It was good to be home again.

Samantha did not want her Mother waiting on her, so she tried to do things for herself to take some of the burden off of Cindy. Her Mother had always been the anchor that had kept the family afloat. Looking after Samantha was just part of the deal. She wanted her daughter to heal completely from her injuries and intended to do her best to make it happen. Samantha had grown pretty independent in the past few years and wasn't about to be 'babied' in any way, shape or form!

Tom called the house after Samantha had been home for a couple of days. 'How are things going?' he asked Cindy. "Samantha is getting along well and getting back to her old happy self', Cindy continued. Tom smiled as Cindy told him about Samantha's progress thus far. He asked to talk to Samantha after a while. Samantha told Tom that he could come over the next afternoon if he would like to. Tom agreed and told Samantha that he would see her tomorrow.

Samantha had taken every opportunity to rest that she could get. Dr. Hin had told her that rest was the most important thing to help her get better, along with her physical therapy treatments. These were the only ways for Samantha to get herself back to better health once again. Once she got back to her normal routines again, she expected to be feeling a million times better than she had in weeks. Samantha longed for the day when she could drive again. With this goal in mind, she set out to meet it!

Cindy had asked Tom to stay for supper the next afternoon. It would be a surprise for Samantha. Cindy hoped that Samantha wouldn't be upset over it. Besides, it was the least she could do when Tom had been there for the both of them through all of the hectic days that were behind them. Tom was a nice young man and Cindy intended to invite him over as often as he would like to come or as often as Samantha would allow it. Cindy was preparing Salisbury steak that night for supper. Samantha helped to set the table as her Mother cooked the meal. 'Be sure to set an extra place at the table' Cindy told Samantha. 'I've invited Tom to stay and eat with us tonight'. Samantha smiled to hear her Mother's invitation and hurried to set another place at the table.

Samantha hurried the best that she could to answer the door when Tom arrived at the house. 'Hello, young lady'. 'Hello' Samantha said shyly. 'Come in' she told him as she closed the front door behind him. Tom was so handsome that Samantha could hardly contain her smile that afternoon. She felt as if she would melt into a puddle on the floor in front of him. Why was she so nervous? Samantha and Tom had known each other for years so these crazy bursts of 'goofiness' should not be happening to her.

After Samantha and Tom studied together for a while, they took a break from her school work to eat supper. Samantha was not expecting her brothers to 'grill' Tom with '20 questions' that evening. But he was a good sport and fired the answers right back at them! Samantha hid her embarrassment very well from her brothers and of course, Tom that night. She intended to reprimand the both of them later on, and sharply! Samantha quickly changed the subject to Tom's school classes. She breathed a sigh of relief to hear him tell everyone about his schedule this year. 'My classes have been going well' Tom told Samantha. 'I've also tried out for 'South Pacific', 'the musical production this year at school'. The thought of Tom's voice made the butterflies in Samantha's stomach do a dance. Snorts from her siblings made her think of other things to talk about before they had the chance to embarrass her again.

After supper, Samantha helped Cindy clear the table then gathered up the homework that she and Tom had begun to work on earlier. She wasn't real concerned about catching up with her classmates in her studies at school. Samantha was a good student and with Tom's help, would be 'up to speed' in no time. No worries here! English lessons were a breeze for Samantha but Algebra was a different story all together! Thank goodness for Tom's help in that subject.

Tom noticed the time and told Samantha that he should get going so he could work on his own homework. He thanked Cindy for supper and told Samantha to call him if she needed his help again with her school work. Tom gave Samantha a hug before he left and also a peck on the cheek. 'Thank-you Tom', Samantha said sweetly as she closed the door behind him. Next on the agenda, chew on her brothers for asking a million questions of Tom! 'You guys are something else' she told them accusingly. 'Why do you ask such things? Samantha asked her older siblings. Scott replied, 'We're just looking out for you, Samantha'. Samantha thanked the two of them and went about tidying up the living room. In a way, it was kind of sweet that her brothers were looking out for her. She was thankful for the both of them, even though they sometimes went a little 'overboard'.

Samantha retired to the sofa bed that she had come to know so well. She cuddled up with a book she had found in her room that she had forgotten about. When her eyes began to feel heavy, Samantha turned on a movie for a while. It didn't take long before she was out. Her recovery had been long and there still was a ways to go yet before she would be given a clean bill of health from Dr. Hin. Strong-willed Samantha would not be kept down, especially from her young life at High School.

Chapter fifteen

A whole year had passed since Samantha's accident and according to Dr. Hin, she had healed very well. Samantha was now a High School senior. She was excited about the year ahead of her. It promised to be a great first semester and Samantha couldn't wait to see her friends again. Tom had left for college in Michigan a few weeks ago. The two didn't talk as often as Samantha would have liked too. Tom had not yet revealed his feelings to Samantha but he hoped to see her over the Labor Day weekend. It was time for him to confess his feelings to Samantha.

Samantha had signed herself up for a full schedule at school this year. She hoped to keep herself busy with her studies and her part-time job at the convenience store in town. Scott and Charles had chosen to go to the community college, in order to be close to the farm in case their Mother needed them. The two brothers shared an apartment near campus. Cindy was content with her sons having their own space as long as they promised to visit once a week.

Samantha was still very proud of her car and took painstaking measures to keep it looking like new. And so it was, until one day at school! Someone had backed into it while she was inside at one of her classes. Samantha had come outside during a break between classes and seen the damage. A young lady had waited for her near her car. 'I'm so sorry', the young girl said. 'I was in a hurry and didn't look behind me' she continued. Samantha went inside to call their parents and went back outside to console the girl until the parents arrived. 'It will be O.K.' Samantha told the girl.

After all was said and done, the damage turned out to be minimal on Samantha's car. 'I felt bad for the young girl, Mom' Samantha told Cindy. Cindy told Samantha that she was sure that she had learned to be more careful next time. Cindy told Samantha that she would call the insurance company about the damage, tomorrow.

Now that it was just the two of them, Cindy prepared smaller meals for herself and Samantha. The two women sat down to a delicious grilled chicken salad and some wheat bread from the bakery downtown. Once in a while, Cindy invited Scott and Charles over for supper. That is, when they had the time! The brothers kept themselves tied up with their school work and their jobs. It was hard to get them both together at the same time anymore.

When the time had come for Cindy to finally go through William's things, she had decided to give most of his clothes to a charity. She had kept only a few of her husband's personal belongings. Cindy still treasured her beautiful locket and the sweet heartfelt letter that William had written for her. But most of all, Cindy held tight to the memories of her wonderful, loving husband. She had compiled cards, photographs and some keepsakes into a scrapbook to help keep William close to her heart. Sometimes, she had wished that William was still here with her but knew that the Lord had needed him more than she had, whether she liked it or not.

It had been good therapy for Cindy to take care of Samantha after her accident. It kept Cindy's mind busy as she too healed from the loss of her husband. Samantha had turned out to be a fighter, just like her Dad was. Cindy was pleased that Samantha had fought to get better after the accident. It would have been devastating had her injuries been even more serious than they already were.

Thanksgiving was fast approaching. Cindy thought it would be nice to invite Linda and Susie over for the big meal this year. Cindy enjoyed having company over to the house. She loved to entertain and it was time for a change! So she had decided to invite different friends over during select holiday celebrations. Samantha would lend a hand where she could and now wasn't any exception!

Samantha was looking forward to seeing Melissa over the Holiday break. She also had planned to see Tom when he returned home for the Holidays. They had missed each other during the

Labor Day weekend, so had planned to get together at Christmas. As Samantha sat at her desk that evening after supper, she jotted down the names of a few colleges that she was interested in. Now was a good time to start thinking about her future education plans. Tom was studying elementary education in Michigan and Samantha thought that maybe she might look into that field also. It was all too much to think about tonight. She had been running non-stop all week and she was just about to fall apart. Then, Samantha got the sweetest phone call. It was Tom on the other end and she beamed with joy just to hear his voice! 'Are we going to get together during break?' Tom asked Samantha. 'Sure, I'd love that', Samantha gushed.

The volunteer program at the hospital had peaked Samantha's interest while she had been a patient there. Tom asked her about her plans for school and she told him about the different interests she had. And the volunteer program was brought up during their conversation too. 'You would be a great volunteer, Samantha', Tom told her. 'I just might look into that a little more' Samantha said to him. It was beginning to get dark and Samantha needed to study, so the two friends said 'good-bye'.

When she was finished studying, Samantha found her pajamas and said her prayers. She thanked God for her great group of friends and her family. She prayed for herself too, even though she always prayed for others first. She just wanted to make sure that she would choose the right college. This would be a major step in her young life and she wanted to be sure that she was doing the right thing!

After prayers, Samantha went to sleep. Exhausted and weary, she fell into her deep sleep, the kind of sleep that brought dreams to her. The dreams of weddings, flowers and beautiful bridesmaids haunted her sleep time once again. Her dream seemed to go on and on as Samantha slept. In her dream, the flowers she carried were some of the most beautiful roses she had ever seen! Her Dad was there with her, walking down the aisle of the Church as everyone stared at the lovely woman before them. Samantha smiled with love and adoration for the people who had come to share this day with her.

The dream went on and on as once she arrived at the Alter, she could not see her Groom's face. Samantha awoke with a start. She realized that she had been dreaming and wiped the tears from her eyes as she had done many times before. Samantha tried to go back to sleep but the dream just kept re-playing in her mind. It had been so real she wondered what it all meant! Samantha climbed out of bed and went downstairs to get a glass of water and came back upstairs to her bed. She hoped to get some sleep now that she was in a clear frame of mind again.

Little did Samantha know, but she would one day find the reason for her dream and it would be a wonderful, pleasant surprise to her as well!

Breakfast the next morning was quick. Cindy and Samantha were heading to the supermarket to get their 'Thanksgiving feast' supplies and groceries. On the way to the store, Samantha asked her Mother about dreams and their meanings. 'Why do you ask?' Cindy asked her daughter. 'I've been having a dream that I'm getting married, but I cannot see the Groom's face', Samantha explained. Cindy told Samantha that her sub-conscious mind was working over-time. She then explained that she had been through a lot of things in the past two years. 'That could be a big part of it', Cindy told her.

Cindy's explanation made some sense to Samantha but she still was curious about her repetitive dream. She tried to keep herself busy with helping her Mother get the house ready for company to visit them. The big day was just a couple of days away and Samantha was happy that she would see her friends, Tom and Melissa, again. She couldn't wait to talk with Melissa and get her up to date on all the news.

As Samantha helped her Mother prepare the big meal, she thought how her friends had always been an important part of her life. She couldn't help but wonder if some of her friends would remain in Swanton after they graduated from High School. Her hopes to go to a college in Michigan were strong, but Samantha worried about leaving her Mother alone. She would miss her terribly although she knew that she needed to get her education. Cindy would be alright. Her sons were close by and the neighbors were always willing to help if she needed anything. Yes, Samantha knew that her Mother would be O.K., but would she herself survive the change?

Linda and Susie arrived at the house early to help out with the meal. The table was beautiful when the women finished setting it for dinner. As expected, Samantha's brothers were almost late. They arrived just as the food was being brought to the table and Samantha scolded the both of them for being 'tardy'! But, they were together and that was all that mattered right now anyway.

Linda was asked to say 'Grace' over the food and was glad to oblige. Once the prayer was said, the food was passed around and the meal began. Nobody had better go away from the table hungry today! It would be a shame to miss out on any of the delicious food that had been set before them! Samantha quizzed her brothers about their girlfriends but got no answers out of either one of them. Both were tight lipped about the female friends in their lives.

After the big meal was eaten and the dishes cleaned up, everyone sat in the living room to visit. It was nice to have someone to visit with, Samantha thought to herself as she and Susie talked together. Cindy mentioned to Linda that she might get her Christmas tree while the boys were around to help her next weekend. 'It is such a chore to even get a big tree inside the doorway, let alone chopping it down by myself', Cindy told her friend. It would be a great time to get their tree while Cindy had plenty of help. Samantha offered to help her Mom over the weekend with decorating for the Holiday Season. The tradition at the farm was to decorate after the Thanksgiving Holiday and Cindy intended to continue the tradition as long as she was able to.

Just about everything got some sort of decoration for the Christmas Holiday, whether it was a picket fence, the mailbox or just a shrub. Everything at the farm was decorated to show the family's Holiday spirit. Samantha just shook her head at her

Mother when she asked her to decorate the 'Well House' too! 'I want this place to be the most festive that it's ever been', Cindy told her children.

It warmed Cindy's heart to have her family around her now, especially since William's passing. The closeness of her family helped to ease her loneliness for William. Linda suggested that they all go Christmas shopping together this year. Cindy agreed that it was a fabulous idea! The two younger women didn't have much to say, at least at this point anyway. It was too early for them to think about Christmas shopping yet.

Linda and Susie left after their visit on Thanksgiving Day. Since Samantha's accident, the four women had become closer friends and there seemed to be a much stronger bond between them. Samantha thought about what a good friend that Linda had been to her Mother. She had been there for Cindy no matter the situation or circumstance.

When the alarm clock went off the next morning, Samantha awoke with a start. She had been dreaming about sandy beaches and a beautiful blue ocean. She stretched and smiled as she climbed out of her bed. Melissa would be here today for a visit! She could hardly wait to see her friend, so Samantha hurried to get ready. She would be picking Melissa up at the train station in town at 11:15 this morning.

Samantha hummed a Christmas tune as she got ready to meet her friend. She loved the Christmas Holiday with her family but it would not ever be the same without her Dad around. As Samantha put on a bit of make-up, she thought about how Tom had once said that she was beautiful. She brushed it off as Tom just being nice to her. Anyway, Samantha was glad that her two friends would be visiting soon!

When Samantha arrived at the train station, she didn't wait long before Melissa's train arrived. The girls shrieked with excitement to see one another once again. Melissa ran to Samantha and threw her arms around her and hugged her tight. There was so much to talk about it seemed the two girls were chatting before they even made it to Samantha's car!

The two best friends talked and laughed all the way to the restaurant, where they sat down to get some lunch. It was nice to see Melissa and Samantha made sure that Melissa knew it. "I've missed you, Melissa', Samantha told her. "Me too', Melissa said as she took a bite of her sandwich. The two girls talked while they enjoyed their lunch and each other's company. After lunch, Samantha drove Melissa to her aunt's house, where she would be visiting for a few days.

When it was time to say 'good-bye' again, Samantha hugged Melissa and told her how much she loved and missed her. Without breaking down into tears, Melissa managed to tell Samantha the same. They had been apart for so long it was difficult to part ways again so soon! 'I promise I will try to write to you', Melissa half cried out to Samantha as she walked up the sidewalk to her aunt's porch. 'Me too', Samantha called back to her friend as she climbed into her car.

The miles between Samantha and Melissa hadn't affected their friendship at all. The two friends were still as close as two sisters, maybe even closer than that! The girls had been friends since kindergarten and hadn't been apart very often since then, until now! Samantha pondered their friendship and was happy she had met Melissa. They had spent so many happy years together as best friends.

Chapter sixteen

It was now Sunday morning. Samantha would be getting a visit from Tom today. He would be home for a break from college for a week. Samantha was looking forward to seeing Tom again. He had always been so easy to talk to and he was pretty easy on the eyes too! Samantha thought maybe she shouldn't be thinking about him in that way but maybe she was just admiring the handsome young man that he was.

After breakfast, Samantha went upstairs to get ready for the day ahead. She had wanted to dress warmly and look nice at the same time today. Could it be that she wanted to catch Tom's eye too? She settled for a pair of jeans and a pretty sweater before running back downstairs again.

'How do I look Mom? Samantha asked her Mother. 'You look beautiful' was her reply to her daughter. 'Samantha, you could wear a bag and you would still be lovely', Cindy told her. Samantha told her Mother that she always told her that and went about helping tidy up the house.

Tom arrived at Samantha's house around 11:00 A.M. He quickly hugged Samantha and then hugged her Mother. 'You both look pretty today' Tom told them as they all gathered in the living room. Tom and Samantha sat and caught up on the latest news. Then, Tom asked Samantha if she would like to get some lunch with him. Cindy told Samantha that she could go to lunch with Tom when she overheard Tom ask her. Cindy didn't mean to 'eavesdrop' on their conversation, it just so happened, that she was coming in to offer them something to drink! Samantha grabbed her purse and a light jacket. She then kissed her Mother 'good-bye'.

It had been a while since Samantha had been on a date but she wasn't at all nervous with Tom sitting by her side. When they arrived at the small diner, Tom opened the door for Samantha and escorted her to a table near the window. While waiting for their lunch, the friends talked about many things. One of which, was their hopes and dreams for the future.

Both seemed to have similar aspirations and hopes for their young lives, marriage, children, etc. etc. It all sounded surreal to Samantha, almost as if she were in a dream or something. How could it be that they shared so many things in common? Samantha truly felt that Tom just may have been sent from Heaven! The pizza had finally arrived and Samantha felt a funny sort of relief as they shared lunch together.

The pizza was as delicious as they had been told. After they finished, Tom asked, 'Would you like to share a Hot Fudge Sundae with me'? 'Sure, why not?' Samantha replied with a grin. Tom smiled back at her and waved the waitress over to their table. Tom fidgeted while they waited for their ice cream. His nerves seemed to be getting the best of him today. He thought to himself, 'it's now or never' and decided to tell Samantha how he felt about her.

He began with, 'Samantha'. She looked up at him in response. 'I think you are one of the sweetest girls that I've met', he began. 'I was wondering if you might like to be my girlfriend'. Samantha sat quietly for a moment going over what Tom had said to her. By now, their ice cream had arrived and still, Samantha had not answered Tom's question.

Samantha sat and stared at the ice cream. She was still in shock from the question that Tom had asked. 'Will you be my girlfriend?' Tom asked again nervously. This time, he got his answer. 'Yes' was all that Samantha could muster for the moment. Satisfied with her answer, Tom got up and went over to Samantha and kissed her, but this time it was on the lips! Samantha gushed from ear to ear then took a bite of the sundae.

When Tom sat back down, he confessed to Samantha that he wasn't sure that she was going to say 'yes' to his question. 'I was a basket of nerves', he told her. Relieved, Tom dug into the huge sundae before them. After they finished their dessert, the new couple drove to the mall to gander at the Christmas displays in the atrium.

The lights and decorations made the time spent with Tom that afternoon, even more special for Samantha. She was still having a hard time believing that they now were a couple! What a great Christmas this was going to be this year! Samantha could hardly contain her happiness at this moment nor did she want to. As they walked through the mall, they held hands. Each of them nervous but glad to be together, at last!

As they walked, they talked about Christmas wishes and their new relationship as boyfriend and girlfriend. They stopped for a moment at the fountain. Tom threw some coins into the flowing water and made a wish. As he turned back towards Samantha, he embraced her and gave her a kiss. They both knew that his wish had already been granted!

Cindy was happy about Samantha's budding relationship with Tom. Samantha was bashful about talking with her Mother about boys but found it easy to talk with her about Tom. 'He's a great young man', Cindy had told Samantha. He had been raised in a Christian family and was well-liked by many. Cindy was thankful that her daughter had met such a nice young man.

Tom had gone back to school in Michigan. He would be back in Swanton before Christmas to spend the Holidays with his family. Samantha could hardly wait to see him again! He was all that she could think about lately. She had not ever felt this way about a boy before and wondered if this was how it was supposed to be. It didn't matter, because Samantha missed Tom terribly and couldn't wait to be near him again.

Warmth and a sense of security surrounded Samantha while she was with Tom. Had she truly been bitten by the 'love bug'? She grinned to herself as she wrapped a lovely scarf that she had bought for her Mom as a Christmas gift. It was time for Samantha to think about getting ready for bed. It had been an eventful day and it was time for some much-needed rest!

Samantha concentrated on her final exams at school for the next couple of weeks. It seemed to help her to keep her mind busy. She studied real hard and had asked Cindy to quiz her, a couple of times, on some History and Economics questions. Cindy had told her that she would do just fine on her tests. 'Don't doubt yourself', her Mother had said reassuringly. Samantha told her Mother, 'I get a mental block and then I get nervous'. 'You'll do fine', Cindy reiterated.

Cindy hugged Samantha and kissed her forehead. 'Good-night, Samantha' she said as she herself, made her way upstairs for the night. Samantha retired to her room shortly thereafter. She fell asleep thinking how lucky she was to have a wonderful family. And, a new love interest by the name of Tom Holden! Her feelings for Tom had blossomed in a very short time but she knew that those feelings were true and just.

Inevitably, the forecast was for a white Christmas. This delighted Samantha because she and Tom were hoping to go sledding with friends over the winter break. During the last week at school before the break, many students exchanged gifts or cards. Some took pictures for their scrapbooks or photo albums. There was a menagerie of blissful Holiday spirit that flowed through the school that week.

What a wonderful time of year for all who believed! Samantha sat and thought about the very first Christmas, the night when Jesus was born. She realized that Mary had actually wrapped the very first Christmas present! Baby Jesus! How sweet it would have been to see him lying in his manger that night. Oh, what a fabulous night that must have been for Joseph, Mary, the Three Wise Men and the shepherds!

Samantha hurriedly finished wrapping the gifts that she had picked out for her brothers. She hoped that they would like what she had chosen for each of them. Samantha was happy to have her own spending money now. Her job at the convenience store had turned out to be a good one. She really liked her boss and the hours she worked weren't too bad either!

Samantha hoped to get an easy schedule through the holidays, so that she could spend plenty of time with her family. And let's not forget about spending time with her new 'beau', Tom! Samantha sat down on her bed and reflected back to the time when she and Tom had met in grade school. Tom would pull her pigtails in class when the teacher wasn't looking. Another memory came to her as she sat and reminisced about her younger days. She remembered when she took Tom's football from him when he wouldn't stop teasing her. She couldn't remember ever giving back to him either!

That was enough of walking down 'Memory Lane'. They had been children then and were just having a good time. Now, things were just a little more serious than 'pigtails and pigskins' in their young adult lives!

Samantha put the wrapping supplies away and carried her gifts downstairs to put them under the Christmas tree. The family tree was exceptionally beautiful this year. Or could it be that it was beautiful because Samantha was so happy? It didn't matter. It was going to be a wonderful holiday at the Weston home. On that thought, the doorbell rang so Samantha hurried to answer the door.

There stood Tom, grinning ear to ear and holding one of the most gorgeous gifts that Samantha had ever seen! 'This would be for you, young lady' Tom told her. 'And you are not allowed to open it until Christmas!' Tom finished. 'If you say so sir', said Samantha as she shut the front door. 'You are so sweet', Samantha told him as he leaned over to give her a kiss. 'I try', Tom told her as he sat down on the sofa.

The big Holiday was just days away. This meant that Samantha would need to wait to open the gift from Tom. She was sure it was worth the wait!

Christmas day had arrived! Samantha climbed out of bed to see if her Mother was awake. The smell of coffee wafted up the steps so Samantha knew that Cindy was indeed up and already beginning her day. Samantha crept downstairs to see if her Mother needed a hand in the kitchen. 'Good-morning Mom' Samantha said. 'Merry Christmas, honey', Cindy replied. Samantha could smell the ham baking in the oven. She asked her Mother if she could help peel potatoes. 'Sure, if you'd like', Cindy answered.

'You're up early today', Samantha told her Mother. 'I couldn't sleep' Cindy told her. 'I kept thinking about your Dad and it made me restless' she continued. 'I miss Dad too', Samantha told her Mother. Cindy continued with, 'I'm sure that he's smiling down on us and knows that we'll all be O.K.'. 'I believe it too', Samantha said. The two women hugged and continued preparing the Christmas meal.

'What time are my brothers coming over?' Samantha asked her Mother. 'I asked them to be here at 2:00 P.M.' Cindy told her. Although both of them knew that Scott and Charles were anything but 'on time', they agreed that they would probably arrive around 1:45 P.M. It was to be expected from those two 'lazy-bones'!

Surprisingly, the brothers arrived somewhat early for a change. They had even brought some type of dessert from the bakery! Samantha was in shock at the two of them. They had even dressed up in some of their nicest clothes this time. The only thing that Samantha wasn't surprised about was the fact that they had brought a goofy movie over to watch later on. Not particularly fond of comedies, Samantha turned her nose up at the movie they had chosen. 'I'll visit with Tom while you are watching your silly movie', Samantha told her brothers.

Christmas dinner was served right on time and with all the delicious trimmings that came along with a meal of this caliber! Cindy had once more pulled off another fantastic Holiday meal and everyone ate until they could barely move. 'Delicious', Scott had managed to tell his Mother in between bites of food. 'Great' was all that came out of Charles' mouth.

They were all too full to eat dessert yet, so after dishes were done they all sat in the living room. 'Can we exchange gifts now?' Samantha asked her Mother. 'Sure, why not?' she answered. Samantha walked over to the Christmas tree to retrieve the gift that she had bought her Mother and placed it on her lap. As Cindy opened her gift, Samantha snapped a picture of her. 'Samantha, it's beautiful', Cindy said as she gazed upon a lovely salmon colored scarf. She also admired the gifts from her sons.

In turn, the siblings opened their gifts, one by one. 'Thank-you' was said all around the room after everyone opened their gifts. What a great array of unique presents they had chosen for one another! One lone gift sat underneath the tree after all of the family gifts had been opened. It was the gift from Tom that sat alone under the tree. Samantha smiled at the thought of Tom wrapping the gift all by himself.

The 'lone' gift reminded Samantha to run upstairs to retrieve Tom's Christmas present. Scott and Charles sat there and laughed at the movie that they had brought with them. Samantha shook her head at the two goofballs who were her brothers. 'I love you guys', she shouted over the movie to them. 'Yeah' was all they muttered in return to her.

The doorbell rang and rescued Samantha from the 'dumb' movie. She hurried over to answer the door and let Tom inside. 'These are for your Mom', he said as he handed Samantha a bouquet of flowers. 'Mom, Tom brought you a surprise', Samantha called to her Mother in the kitchen. Cindy walked out to greet Tom and to receive the beautiful flowers. 'Thank-you, Tom' she said as she went to find a vase and some water for them.

Samantha greeted Tom with a hug and a kiss then the two sat down for a moment. It seemed to Samantha that Tom was awfully quiet but she didn't mention it to him. She knew that he had been busy lately and blamed his mood on that. The two exchanged gifts at last. Samantha was flabbergasted at her gift from Tom! He had chosen a hand-made musical jewelry box. Inside the box was a pair of pearl earrings.

'Thank-you Tom', she said as she hugged him tight. 'Now, it's your turn' Samantha told Tom. She walked over to get his gift then handed it to him as she sat back down. Inside the pretty Christmas wrap, was a 3-D puzzle of the Empire State Building in New York City. Samantha had heard that Tom enjoyed putting puzzles together, from his Mother. She had also said that he loved history, so she thought he would enjoy the gift of both.

'Who wants pie?' Cindy asked. 'I do', Tom replied. Of course, the goofy brothers both would have some pie too. Samantha hoped that her brothers wouldn't embarrass her in front of Tom. She would just have to keep them busy while Tom was at the house, that's all! She really didn't feel like dealing with their drama today so she tried to keep them away from Tom.

Pie and coffee were served and everyone agreed that Cindy made the best pie around. 'Well, thank-you' she told them. She then told everyone that she still used her Grandmother's recipe. 'I learned when I was a young girl to make Grandma's pie' Cindy told them. Tom asked Samantha if she could bake pies like her Mother did. Her reply was, 'I do my best to try'.

The whole group watched a Holiday special on television after they had enjoyed some dessert. They all enjoyed each other's company until it began to get dark outside. Tom exclaimed that he would be leaving to go his Grandmother's house. He was to meet his family there. So, Tom said his 'good-byes' to everyone and thanked them for their hospitality.

Samantha walked Tom to the door. She thanked him for the gift and he did the same. The couple hugged and kissed 'good-bye', then, Tom went out into the cold, dark night. 'Merry Christmas' he called as he got into his car and drove off. Samantha had been thinking that Tom seemed somewhat distant but blamed it on the rush of the Holidays. Little did she know that he was up to more than just celebrating the Holiday!

Tom frantically drove down Samantha's road to get to his next stop. It certainly wasn't his Grandmother's house and he knew he shouldn't have lied. He had been drawn into the world of drug-dealing while away at College, as a means of making some extra money. Tom knew in his heart of hearts that what he was doing was wrong but he really needed the money. He drove to an old abandoned warehouse where he sat and waited in his car for his buyer. He hadn't waited long before he saw headlights coming down the driveway. Tom breathed a sigh of relief as he saw a nervous-looking man climb out of the car. The man looked around as if to see if the coast was clear, then he proceeded over to Tom's car.

Tom got out of the car and talked with the man before cutting the deal. When he was satisfied that this man was for real, Tom reached into his pocket for the 'goods'. He told the man that this was the 'good stuff' and showed him the bag of drugs. Just as those words came out of Tom's mouth, an unmarked police car drove up from around the side of the old warehouse. Tom had made the deal with an undercover policeman and he had been caught 'red-handed!

Tom was read his rights, then hand-cuffed and put into the back seat of the police cruiser. Tom's immediate thoughts were of his family and how he had let them down. He wondered how he could have been so selfish, and how foolish to even think that he would get away with such a crime. The humiliation alone was devastating and Tom knew that he would pay dearly for this!

When they arrived at the police station, Tom was put into a jail cell and booked for the narcotics charge. He knew that when word got back to Samantha she would be very displeased with him for this horrible crime. His heart sank to think of the consequences that he would need to face, not only with the law but also, with his girlfriend.

When Samantha heard that Tom was in jail, she couldn't believe it! How could her sweet boyfriend have done such a thing? Cindy explained that sometimes, money made you do things that you normally wouldn't do, whether it was right or wrong. Samantha said to her Mom, 'But drugs, Mom?' 'What was he thinking?' she continued.

Samantha tried to put the situation out of her mind. Instead, she kept thinking about what a great Christmas day they had spent together. There was no use dwelling on it but she intended to get to the bottom of this. Even if it meant that she would need to break up with Tom!

Chapter seventeen

Samantha was back at school on January third, but still hadn't heard from Tom. She wondered if he was trying to avoid her because he was embarrassed or maybe he thought that Samantha wouldn't want to talk to him. Whatever the reason, Samantha was still fuming over Tom's actions. She wasn't sure that she was ready to talk to him yet anyway! She didn't want to hold a grudge but this was serious. Could she trust Tom after this foolish choice he had made?

Samantha managed to keep up on her studies over the next few weeks and was actually doing well at school this semester. She and Cindy had discussed a graduation party next summer but hadn't worked out the details yet. Keeping her mind occupied was foremost on Samantha's mind. She wondered to herself if Tom was planning on contacting her. Or would he hide away from her until she approached him about his predicament?

Just when she thought that she would never hear from Tom, he called her and asked if she could meet him somewhere to talk. Samantha was hesitant at first, but eventually agreed to meet Tom for coffee. Samantha was nervous about seeing Tom after all this time but she knew that they needed to talk about this.

They met at 1:00 o'clock at the coffee shop downtown. Both were at a loss for words at first. Tom spoke first after a few moments of awkward silence. 'Samantha, 'I know that I've done an awful thing but please know I am deeply sorry about this', he pleaded. 'I am in a drug control counseling program twice a week'. "I am also paying court costs'. He continued to tell Samantha how he had learned a lesson from all of this. A very important valuable lesson!

Samantha sat quietly as he poured his heart out to her. When he had pleaded his case, he asked Samantha, 'Can you ever forgive me?' She looked up at Tom and answered, 'You have broken my trust in you'. 'It's going to take some time for us to get through this whole thing', she continued. 'I know, Samantha' he said as he stared at his cup of coffee. He looked up at her and asked, 'Can you ever forgive me?'

Samantha thought for a moment or two then answered Tom with, 'I believe that we can work on it'. Neither could change what had happened but there was an opportunity to learn from this situation that he had brought upon himself. Tom couldn't contain his happiness at Samantha's answer. 'You are the greatest, most understanding girl that I have ever met!' 'I promise that I will do my best to put all of this behind me', he muttered.

'Good answer, Tom Halson', Samantha told him. The young couple sat and talked about other events in their lives and set aside the 'drug' issue for the time being. Deep down, Samantha knew that Tom was a good person. She hoped nothing would ever happen in their lives like this again. Part of her was embarrassed for Tom and part of her was angry at him. This type of drama in their lives was not welcome especially when they were just getting to know one another.

Spring was merely weeks away. Tom would begin his community service as part of his drug rehabilitation sentence. Samantha had faith in Tom that he would put forth an effort to clear his good family name. His sentence had been less severe because Tom had given the authorities some names of his suppliers. He vowed to clean up his act and to talk to young children about the dangers of drugs every chance that he had.

Samantha remained focused on school and her grades. Graduation was first on her mind and she intended to get that diploma, no matter what it took! Tom continued to participate in his community service projects until his time had been served. The Judge had been more than fair with him, so Tom decided that he would try and help others out at their community service appointments. It was the least that he could do to help out others that had been in his shoes and were also trying to learn from their mistakes.

The last day of school for the seniors at 'Montgomery High School' would be Tuesday, May eighth. Samantha was very excited to be in this graduating class. The 'Class of 1982' was 150 classmates strong, all eager to make their marks on the world in one way or another. Samantha thought about studying social work or something similar. She wanted to keep her options open, in case she changed her mind down the road.

Nonetheless, Samantha was excited to look forward to her future, not only in her college education but possibly with Tom also. She knew that Tom was worried about what Samantha felt about him, now that he had committed a crime. She set her mind to forgive him and to proceed with their relationship.

Tom seemed sincere about his willingness to turn his life around, so Samantha trusted her faith in Tom and in her Savior to keep him on the 'straight and narrow'! It meant so much to Tom to be earning Samantha's trust again. He had worked really hard to keep his faith and had begun going to Church once again. Tom knew he needed strength, not only from his own will but from God's love around him also. His guidance was real important to Tom at this turning point in his life!

Samantha's graduating class had all been fitted for their caps and gowns, which meant graduation day wasn't far off. It seemed sad to Samantha that she may not ever see some of her friends again. She thought about the many different directions that certain students would be taking. Some would be doctors, some lawyers even some might be policemen or women.

It was hard at this point to know where any of Samantha's classmates would end up. She simply hoped that all would get the chance to pursue their dreams. Samantha's Mother had taught her children to 'savor the moment', for it would pass before your very eyes. Cindy was a smart woman and had many words of wisdom and sage advice.

Samantha said a prayer for her fellow classmates that all would find happiness and above all, love. This was the least that she could do for them. Another thought came to Samantha's mind, a memory of kindergarten graduation. The caps and gowns, all in much smaller sizes and the cute hand-made diplomas brought a smile to Samantha's face, as she remembered that day not so long ago!

Cindy had just come to the realization that her 'baby' would be graduating soon. She decided she would discuss the graduation party with Samantha so they could get some plans in the works. Cindy hoped that Samantha would have a future with Tom. She knew that he was doing his best to keep on the 'straight and narrow' but in the back of her mind, there was a 'what if' lurking there. She set those thoughts aside and busied herself making a guest list for Samantha's party. She was thankful for her family, whom she had taught strong values and morals, those which were sometimes uncommon in this day in age.

Samantha had invited Tom for supper and a movie on Saturday. He told Samantha that he would be at the senior center helping out until 5:00 that afternoon. He asked if he could come over a little later on, maybe around 7:00 P.M. Samantha agreed that would be fine and told Tom that she would see him then. She busied herself cleaning the house and helping out in the kitchen until then.

After a meal of stuffed pork chops and escalloped potatoes, Tom and Samantha sat and enjoyed a movie, some sort of comedy that she had rented at the video store. It was as if Tom and Samantha hadn't been apart for long at all. They sat and appreciated each other's company for the first time in a while. The couple laughed at the actor's antics until they had tears in their eyes. It was good to relax and be a happy couple again!

Tom felt in his heart that he and Samantha were meant to be together and he had pledged to her to make sure that it stayed that way. Samantha hugged Tom and he leaned over to give her a kiss as they said good-night at the front door. Both knew that God had brought them together again. There seemed to be some sort of plan for the two of them and they were determined to find out together what that plan was.

Graduation day had arrived. Samantha was in her room putting on her new dress, when Cindy came in to admire how pretty she looked. 'Thanks, Mom', Samantha told her. 'Samantha, 'You have grown into a beautiful, smart young woman, and I am so very proud of you', Cindy told her daughter. 'Thank-you, Mom', she told her.

'Mom, 'Had it not been for you and Dad, 'who knows what my life would have been like', Samantha replied. She knew that Cindy and William had done their very best with their children and was thankful for that. Samantha hugged and kissed her Mother, then finished getting ready for graduation. 'Mom, 'you may want to bring some extra tissues with you'. 'I'll be singing a song tonight', Samantha told her with a smile.

Cindy, Charles, Scott and Grandma Berta sat as close as possible to the stage in order to see Samantha graduate with her classmates. They wanted to be sure they would be able to get some good pictures of Samantha receiving her diploma.

You could feel the excitement in the air that evening, not only from the graduating seniors but also from their family and friends that had gathered here. This monumental day meant that childhood was over and a new life awaited each one of them. Cindy glanced at her program that held the names of every student. When she found Samantha's name, she pointed it out to Grandma Berta. 'Well, I always knew that Samantha was a smart one', Grandma said. Just then, the processional music began and the students started filing into the auditorium. It was time for them to receive their diplomas, at last! Every student looked happy to be in this very moment in their young lives. Cindy wondered what might be going through their minds as they each took their places on the big stage that evening.

As the last of the students sat down, the audience quieted down. All that was heard was a very quiet series of whispers across the large room. As usual, the Principal and many faculty members spoke to the large crowd, before the diplomas were handed out. But first, Samantha was asked to come to the front to sing her song. As her name was announced, Cindy thought that she might fly right out of her chair. She was very proud for Samantha as she clapped and cheered for her.

The Christian song that Samantha had chosen was an upbeat song that told about love and life lessons and growing up into an adult. When the song was finished, there didn't appear to be a dry eye in the house! Samantha received a standing ovation for her rendition of the popular song and bowed for the cheering crowd. Cindy could not have been any prouder of her daughter than at that very moment! As she took another bow, then returned to her seat, Samantha took a deep breath and felt relieved for her song to be over with. Her nerves had almost gotten the best of her but she had managed to keep it under control.

The evening was moving along fairly well and finally, the Biology teacher, Mr. Case, approached the podium to present the students with names beginning with the letter 'W'. At last, it would soon be Samantha's turn to shine! After a few other students were called, she heard Samantha Annette Weston called and walked over to get her long-awaited diploma. The grin on her face told how happy she was to be here at this place in her life.

A wave or two was given as she bowed and smiled to her fan club in the audience. As she walked back to her seat, Samantha heard, 'Way to go young lady' and knew that Tom was somewhere out there in the vast array of people. She grinned to herself and sat down with her now 'prized possession'. This moment had been one that she had waited for all of her life and she was savoring every moment of it!

This was most definitely, a most memorable evening. Samantha hoped once again, for the very best for her fellow classmates as she waited for the final few to receive their rewards for a 'job well-done'. Yes, indeed the future was full of promise and possibilities for each and every one of these young people. As they walked out of this auditorium on this very night, they would be entering a new world of discovery and hope!

Samantha stood in the lobby afterward and greeted family and friends who all had good wishes of luck and happiness for her. Pictures were taken of all who wanted and memories were made that night. Some that would not soon be forgotten. Tom made his way through the crowd to find Samantha. He found her talking with her Grandmother and brothers. Tom gave her a big hug and handed her a lovely bouquet of flowers. She thanked him and asked him to pose with her for a picture.

Cindy snapped several pictures of the family with Samantha, but especially of her and Tom. Cindy had a good feeling about this relationship. She knew in her heart that this just might be a 'match made in Heaven'. She prayed that she was right and hugged the two of them tight before getting ready to go home that evening.

Tom had offered to drive Samantha home when she was ready. He wanted to talk to her about their summer plans on the way to her house. Now that the 'drug thing' was behind them, it was important for Samantha to tell Tom about her feelings for him. She felt it was time to let him know how she had grown to love him. More than anyone she had ever known!

It was a gorgeous summer night, so the couple drove to the park outside of Swanton. Tom asked Samantha if she would like to go for a walk after he parked the car. Samantha agreed that was a great idea so the two of them started on their way. They hadn't walked far when Tom pulled Samantha close and kissed her. He then told her, 'I'm so grateful that you have stuck by me, after all that I have put you through!' He continued with, 'You don't know what it means to me to have someone like you in my life'.

Samantha stepped back a step, then replied, 'Everyone deserves a second chance and you are no exception'. Tom put his arm around her and kissed Samantha again. He was the happiest man on the planet to have Samantha by his side on this night of new beginnings. They continued on, hand in hand into the clear summer night.

Soon, it would be time for Samantha to move to her College campus in Michigan. She had spent many an hour sorting all of the things she would need at school. She was tired of the whole thing and sat down on her bed to rest for a moment. Her Mother came in to see how things were going with the packing situation. 'I'm tired, Mom'! 'I don't have a clue what to take with me and it's making me crazy', she told her Mother.

Cindy helped Samantha to organize everything that she would need while she was away at school. A sigh of relief from Samantha was all the thanks that Cindy needed! It had been another long day and the thought of sleep was a welcome one that night to the young college student. Cindy was somewhat apprehensive about letting Samantha move away to college but knew that she would be O.K. on her own. It would surely be an adjustment for the both of them because they had not been away from each other since Samantha was born! A new experience awaited both Cindy and Samantha in this odd transition.

Cindy reflected a moment on her own college days and remembered her roommates that she had met that first day. To this day, they had remained in contact with one another, even after all this time. As she lay down to go to sleep, Cindy prayed that Samantha too would make life-long friendships while away at college then she drifted off to sleep.

Even though Samantha and Cindy had sorted many things into piles, Samantha's room still looked like a tornado had swept through it! The next morning, they worked together to try and tidy it up before they packed all of Samantha's things into boxes for school. The two women worked most of the day finishing the process of labeling the boxes and folding all of the clothes to be taken away to college.

Chapter eighteen

Finally, the day had arrived to move Samantha to Michigan. Scott had offered to help his sister move and offered his truck to pack everything into. 'I appreciate your help', Samantha told Scott as they loaded the boxes into his truck. 'It's not every day that your little sister moves away to college', Scott chimed as if it were a song on the radio or something!

Unable to take her car to school this year, Samantha would need to rely on her family and friends for transportation back and forth to school. As box after box was loaded unto Scott's truck, it looked as if Samantha would be going on a long trip, a very long trip! It seemed that the truck was full to capacity and still there was more stuff to load.

When they arrived at the school campus, everyone was happy to lend a hand to get Samantha into her dorm before it got late. Again, box after box was unloaded as they hurried to get Samantha's things upstairs and safely inside her room. When it came time for her family to leave her, Samantha hugged each of them and thanked them for their help. Before leaving, Cindy handed Samantha a sealed envelope. Inside it was some extra cash, 'just in case' Cindy said. 'Thank you, Mom', Samantha told her as she hugged her Mother 'good-bye'.

Samantha met her new roommate, Carol, a short time later that afternoon. The two girls had hit it off immediately and had found that they had a lot in common. One of those things was their love of pizza! They found that they were hungry after a long afternoon of moving, so went over to the pizzeria for some supper. While they ate, the two new friends had the chance to get to know one another a little better. When they returned to their dorm, they finished putting away their personal belongings. Otherwise, they would have no place to sleep that night if they hadn't!

'Have you been away from home before?' Samantha asked Carol. 'No, "I've never been away from my family', Carol answered sadly. Samantha told her friend that she too had never been away from her family and was saddened by it. It truly would be a strange new way of life for them, especially when all they had was each other.

It hadn't been long before classes began at the campus. Hurrying from one class to the next became commonplace for Samantha and the other students. She looked forward to many of her new classes, especially her History class! The professor had begun talking about the Roman Empire and Samantha was awestruck over what she was learning so far. This was going to be a good year for Samantha!

Cindy worked to get a 'care package' ready to send to Samantha. She had baked some oatmeal cookies and had packaged them tightly so they would arrive fresh to Samantha. She had also included some postage stamps and some envelopes. Just a subtle hint for Samantha to write to her Grandmother and possibly her Mom! It wouldn't hurt her a bit, thought Cindy as she finished taping up the package.

Although the cafeteria food wasn't bad, Samantha missed her Mom's cooking and couldn't wait to taste it again. She and Carol had begun sharing the packages that their Moms had sent them. It was fun to see what was in each other's surprise boxes! It wouldn't be long until the two girls would be going home for Thanksgiving. They were excited to see their families again and to catch up on all the latest news!

Samantha was also looking forward to seeing Tom on their Holiday break. They had written each other a few times but it wasn't the same as seeing each other in person. Tom had cleaned up his act since she had last seen him and Samantha was proud of him. This new Tom was nice to be around. Samantha grinned to herself as she sat and studied for exams that evening.

Tom had been serious about getting to know Samantha better. And he intended to do just that! He couldn't wait to see his girl again. He had missed her terribly and had so much to talk to her about now. He signed his name to the letter he intended to mail to her the next morning. He grinned when he thought of Samantha's cute smile and her adorable little laugh! His heart was over-flowing with love for her! And there was nobody that could take that away from him. Not anyone at all!

When it came time for Samantha to go home for Thanksgiving, she packed a small bag with a few things that she would need for her stay at home. Cindy arrived around 2:00 P.M. that afternoon to pick Samantha up at her dorm. Samantha told her Mother that her friend, Carol, had left a few hours before to visit with her family over the long weekend. Cindy asked Samantha, 'How do you like being a college girl?' 'It's alright, but I miss you guys, terribly', Samantha replied sadly.

Samantha grabbed her bag off her bed and walked with her Mother outside to her car. It was good to be going home again. She had missed her own bed and couldn't wait to sleep in it again! Cindy and Samantha chatted back and forth on the way back home. Cindy had gotten a raise at work and Linda had been selling a lot of homes lately. It seemed to Samantha that all were doing well in her hometown and this made her happy to be home!

'Grandma Berta and your brothers will be at the house for Thanksgiving dinner', Cindy told Samantha as they drove into the driveway. 'Great, I can't wait to see them', Samantha replied. When Samantha got out of the car, her dog, 'Beau', ran over to greet her. 'Hey, Beau 'How are you?' she asked. She patted him on the head before running inside to take in the smell of 'home'. Samantha hadn't realized how badly she had missed this place. She was so happy to be back in her own bedroom, she jumped up and down on her bed for a moment to celebrate.

For supper tonight, Cindy was making baked chicken and stuffing. Along with that, she was having some home-made applesauce that she had made in the summer. Samantha could hardly wait to sit down to a home-cooked meal tonight! She had waited for what seemed like forever to eat her Mother's cooking again. She was famished and supper time hadn't come none too soon! Samantha felt as if she might just starve before her Mother called her downstairs to eat.

The phone rang shortly after they had finished eating their supper. It was Tom calling for Samantha. 'I'll take it upstairs', Samantha told her Mother. She ran upstairs and picked up the phone, then called to her Mother that she had picked up the other line. 'Tom, how are you', Samantha asked him with a grin. 'I'm better now that I've heard your voice', Tom said. The couple talked for a while until it was time for Tom to go to work.

Samantha had not been able to concentrate very well on her exams, because she had been thinking about Tom so much. But that was a couple of weeks ago. Now that she was home, she could relax and spend time with everyone, including Tom.

Samantha went downstairs to tell her Mother about her conversation with Tom. She told her Mother about her feelings for Tom but Cindy already knew how her daughter felt about her boyfriend. She was pleased that her daughter was a happy young woman and that Tom was faithful to her. While away at college, Samantha had begun eating healthier, so had lost a few pounds. She wondered if Tom would notice the change.

Whenever Samantha was with Tom, she still got that 'giddy' feeling. It seemed to happen more often recently as she became more attracted to this nice young man. Samantha wondered if Tom had those kinds of feelings when he was near her too. And was it normal to be so enamored by someone? Samantha wondered as she dried the supper dishes.

The next morning, Samantha would be going with her Mother to see her friend, Linda. They had been invited over for a small brunch. Samantha was happy to see Susie and Linda again. It had seemed like a long time since she had seen the both of them! Linda once again had cooked a delicious meal for them. Samantha tried some of everything that was put before her. Her stomach was full before she could finish what was on her plate.

After brunch, the women sat and visited with each other for a while. It turned out that Susie had gotten a job at her Mom's office and she enjoyed it. Susie had come out of her shell since she had begun working with her Mom. There was a time when she had been an introvert and extremely bashful!

When it was time to leave for home, Cindy and Samantha went outside and got into their car. Samantha told her Mother she was pleased that she too had been invited to Linda's brunch. A hometown visit with friends was a much-needed break from the daily routines at school, Samantha thought to herself as she and her Mom drove home.

Later that afternoon, Samantha was going over to Tom's house for a visit. She was real excited to see him again. She hurried to help her Mother with some chores before taking a bath that afternoon. Samantha relaxed for a few moments and let the scented warm water soothe her senses.

As she drove to Tom's house, Samantha wondered what the future held for her and Tom. Should she be thinking about a future with him? Or should she wait to see what happened with their relationship? Samantha tried not to think so seriously about the things that she had no control over, but sometimes she couldn't help herself. As she got closer to Tom's house, Samantha checked her makeup in the mirror. Even though Tom said she didn't need it, Samantha still liked to wear just a touch!

She had finally arrived at Tom's house. Samantha walked to the front door and before she could knock, Tom had already opened the door. 'Hi', she said sweetly. 'Hi', Tom replied, before taking her into his arms and kissing her. 'I've missed you', he said as he released her from his arms. 'Me too', Samantha muttered. They took a seat on the huge sofa in the living room. Samantha was at loss for words at first, so she let Tom carry the conversation himself.

After a few moments of small talk, Tom took Samantha's hand and placed it over his heart. She could feel his heart beating rapidly. 'I think my heart skips a beat when I'm with you, Samantha', he told her. She looked into those piercing blue eyes and felt that she could stay there forever. He leaned over and kissed Samantha tenderly. Samantha sat up with a start and asked, 'What about your family?' Tom told her that they had gone to a movie in town. Samantha was uneasy being so close to Tom, especially in his family's home. She trusted him to respect her. But sometimes she wondered if they would be able to keep their promises to one another to remain pure and to remain faithful in their walk with God.

After watching a thriller movie on T.V., Samantha told Tom that she needed to get home before her curfew. The two said 'good-night' and Samantha headed back home. It had been a nice visit with Tom. She hoped that he understood her devotion to him, even though she had made a commitment to herself to remain true to her beliefs and morals. She surely hoped that he respected her for her decision because she intended to respect his choice to remain pure also!

When Samantha arrived home, she found that her Mother was still awake, watching a T.V. show. Samantha sat down with her Mother and talked with her about Tom. Cindy admitted to Samantha that she too had thought about William in the same way when she was young. Samantha asked, 'So this is perfectly normal?' Cindy answered with, 'Yes'. Samantha was relieved to hear her Mother's answer.

Samantha had felt that all she could think about was Tom but now she felt better that she was like everyone else when it came to young love. She and her Mother sat and talked for a while about Samantha's hopes, dreams and the possibility of a future with Tom. It was good to feel close enough to her Mother to discuss her relationship with Tom. The two women sat and talked for a while longer before calling it a night.

Thanksgiving was a Holiday that was cherished by the Weston family, including Grandma Berta. It had been a few years since Grandpa had passed, so she was glad to have someone to spend the day with. Grandma always had a funny story to tell about her childhood days and today was no exception. The family laughed and laughed at her story about her brother jumping off the barn roof into a pile of thistles. 'My Mother picked thorns out of his backside for days', Grandma told them.

As always, Cindy had prepared another fabulous dinner. All of them ate until they thought that they would burst at the seams! Afterward, they all sat down in the living room. Someone mentioned a game of 'Monopoly', but no one wanted to think that hard right now. Instead, they played a game of charades. Scott seemed to be the master of this game because he could guess the clues before anyone else had the chance to try.

Evening had crept up on them so Grandma asked Scott to take her home. Scott obliged and took her home before it got too dark outside. Charles thanked his Mother for the meal then he too headed home for the night. This left Cindy and Samantha alone once again. It didn't matter to either one of them. They enjoyed each other's company anyway! And soon, Samantha would be going back to school again. The extra time spent with her Mother made Samantha happy to come home on break. After finishing the clean-up of the kitchen, the two sat and relaxed for a short while longer. Samantha's excessive yawning triggered Cindy to say that it was time for bed. It had been a great Holiday with the family and the two women needed some rest. So, they went their separate ways to their bedrooms to sleep. The quietness in the house helped to lull the girls to sleep quickly. Into a sleep that slipped them both right into their dreams!

There was a most unusual odor to the air when Samantha stepped out of Cindy's car when they arrived at the college. The pungent smell was heavy in the afternoon air as they made their way to Samantha's dorm. They soon found out there had been a fire just over in the next dorm building down the drive! Samantha was just a little queasy about the whole thing and sat down on her bed for a moment to get her bearings.

She hoped that everyone was O.K.! What a horrible thing to go through. Samantha would find out later that no one was at the dorms when the fire started. Cindy kissed her daughter and told her that she would see her in a few weeks, before heading back to Swanton again. Shortly afterward, Carol arrived back from her Holiday break. She too was surprised about the fire damage at the other dorms. 'I'm glad no one got hurt', Carol told Samantha as they unpacked their bags. 'Me too', Samantha replied. When they finished unpacking, the two friends found an old movie on television to watch. It was a short movie, so when it was over, they went to get a bite to eat. The Christmas Holiday came and went as they always did. Soon, Samantha would be finished with her first year of college. She and Tom had talked about their summer break from school. They had both wanted to go somewhere they hadn't been before.

The young couple had grown very fond of one another in the past year. Tom would write the sweetest letters to Samantha and she tried to do the same. She couldn't bear to be without him for very long. She was so smitten by him that she couldn't see straight! How could one person have such an effect on another human being? Samantha may never find the answer to that particular question, at least not right away!

By the time that spring arrived, Samantha was more than ready for a break. It had been a long first year at school. Her nineteenth birthday waited just around the corner and Samantha felt that the years were passing her by way too quickly! Little did Samantha know, but Tom was planning a special birthday surprise. He wanted to make this birthday a memorable one and he was going to leave 'no stone unturned'.

Tom thought that he might just have the perfect gift for his love, Samantha. And he would do anything for his favorite girl! Samantha had brought Tom a level of happiness into his life that he had never known before. He was proud to say that Samantha was his girlfriend and on this birthday, he wanted everyone else to know how he felt about her!

It was already May, so Tom had only a couple of months left to work on his big surprise for Samantha! He had been working on every detail painstakingly. To put his plan into fruition, Tom thought long and hard about all details of this grand surprise. Mature beyond his years, Tom had faith in his plan and didn't doubt himself for a split second!

The days began flying by quickly, so in between his classes at school, Tom worked on his plans. He was very sure of himself as he told his parents about his plan. Katie offered to help if she could and Tom's Dad offered assistance if Tom needed him. Tom hoped that this all played out as he had planned because this day had to be perfect. He would settle for nothing less!

Chapter nineteen

Samantha's birthday was now just days away but Tom felt that he was ready for the big day. All was in order because he had left nothing to chance. Tom smiled at his efforts as he turned out the light for the night and lay down to go to sleep. His dreams that night were sporadic for his mind drifted back and forth while he slept. Eventually, his dreams were of his beautiful Samantha and his deep love for her.

The next morning, Tom awoke to the sound of the neighbor mowing his lawn. He sat up in his bed and rubbed his eyes, then crawled out of bed. Tom looked out his bedroom window. There was Mr. Adams, preening his lawn for the annual 'July 4th' cookout that his family held each year. Tom yawned and wandered to the kitchen for some fresh coffee.

Katie was already up reading the morning newspaper. Tom sat down with his Mother and a cup of hot coffee at the small kitchen table. After about half a cup of coffee, Tom said to his Mother, 'I've got my plan all worked out Mom'. 'I'm nervous and anxious all at the same time', he told her. Katie responded with, 'It will all work out, Tom'.

As Samantha lay in bed on the morning of her '19th, birthday, many memories flooded her mind. A tapestry of thoughts came of Elementary school, picnics at the park and skating on her Grandmother's pond. These childhood memories were cherished and would always remind Samantha of her younger days. 'Nineteen' seemed old to her but she knew that her life was really just beginning.

Samantha went downstairs and sat with her Mother at the table. She talked with her Mother about time flying by and life creeping up on you. 'And it doesn't stop slipping by you either', Cindy told Samantha. The two shared some home-made wheat toast with strawberry jam for breakfast. 'Happy Birthday, Samantha', piped her Mother as she handed her a small pretty package with a pink bow on it. Samantha opened it and found a bracelet, engraved with her name inside it.

'Mom, it's beautiful', Samantha said as she hugged her Mother. 'Thank-you', she continued. "You're welcome' Cindy told her. The day was moving ahead quickly, so Samantha excused herself to go get ready. She would be going on a special birthday date with Tom later on so she wanted to be presentable. Cindy went about making Samantha a birthday cake although Samantha insisted that she was too old for one.

'Birthdays are meant to be celebrated', had been Cindy's reply to Samantha's protest of a birthday cake. Samantha shook her head and hugged her Mom for her thoughtfulness. 'How do I look?' Samantha asked. 'You look fabulous, Samantha', her Mother said as she mixed up frosting for Samantha's cake. 'Tom will be in awe of your beauty today', Cindy told her. Samantha blushed at her Mother's compliment then sat down to wait for Tom to pick her up.

Tom had gotten up early because the butterflies in his stomach would not let him sleep any longer. He sat down to watch the morning newscast and was half listening to what the newscaster was saying. Tom hoped that Samantha would like her special surprise that he had so painstakingly planned for her. He went upstairs to take a shower and get ready to pick Samantha up for their date. He wanted to get to Samantha's house just a tad early so he could get a jump start on their day.

When he was ready, Tom grabbed some breakfast and sat down to eat it. A bowl of cereal would have to do until he and Samantha got their lunch. After he was finished, Tom brushed his teeth then headed outside to get into his car. He checked that he had not forgotten anything before heading out of the driveway. It was time to go meet his girl.

Samantha had gone back upstairs to change her clothes three times before she decided on the outfit she had on to begin with! She was so nervous today she just could not sit still for any amount of time. She paced back and forth while she waited for Tom to pick her up. Finally, she saw him pull into the driveway and counted to ten to try and calm her frazzled nerves. As he knocked on the front door, Samantha hurried to answer it. 'Hello', Samantha said with a grin. 'Hello' Tom answered her back. The tension was easing the grip it had on Tom, as he kissed Samantha on the cheek.

'Are you ready to go? Tom asked Samantha. 'Yes, let's go', she replied with a smile. She grabbed her purse and took Tom's hand as she called to her Mother, 'good-bye'. Cindy called back from the kitchen, 'You guys have a good time'. The couple went out the door and got into Tom's car. On Samantha's seat was one single red rose. She said to Tom, 'You are so sweet', as they drove away.

Many thoughts ran through Samantha's mind as they drove for what seemed like forever. She wondered what Tom had in store for her on this, her nineteenth birthday. Samantha sat back and tried to relax. Tom asked her if she was O.K. 'I'm Fine', 'I'm just thinking about where we might be going today. 'You'll see soon enough', he told her.

They soon came to a small quaint little town. Samantha sat up straight and took a look around at the pretty town. Tom pulled the car in front of a diner downtown. He walked around the car and let Samantha out of the car. 'Are you hungry', He asked her. 'Yes, I'm famished', Samantha told him. Tom led the way to a table in a quiet corner of the diner and they took their seats. Samantha looked over at Tom and caught a gleam in his eye that she hadn't seen before.

The romantic setting in the diner was refreshing. The young blonde waitress asked if she could get them something to drink. Tom replied with, 'We'll have two iced teas with lemon, please'. The waitress went to get their drinks and the two of them studied their menus as if there would be a test on it later! It turned out they were running a 'special'. Their choices were taco salad or tuna melt with French fries. 'I'll have the taco salad', Samantha said. "I'll have that too', Tom told the waitress.

Tom and Samantha sat quietly as they basked in the glow of the small candle at their table. Tom told Samantha, 'I wanted to bring you someplace that you hadn't been before'. 'This is a great little diner', she answered. Shortly, their lunch arrived and the two feasted on their salads. After a while, the waitress came back and asked if they would like some dessert but neither one had any room for it!

When they were ready to leave, Tom and Samantha went outside and got back into Tom's car. The next destination was a secret also. It didn't take long to get to their next stop. As they got out of the car, Samantha could see that they were at a horse-drawn carriage company. She smiled at Tom's secret and grabbed hold of his hand as they went inside the small office. 'I've got a reservation please', Tom told the girl behind the desk. The woman looked up at Tom and asked his name, then found the reservation on her schedule. 'Yes, let me get your driver for you', she said as she went into another room of her office.

As the driver led Tom and Samantha outside to the carriage, he introduced himself as Henry. He then told them the names of his horses, 'Mac' and 'Joe'. Tom helped Samantha aboard, then he climbed aboard the carriage himself. Henry made sure that they were ready before beginning their ride. Neither Tom nor Samantha had ridden on a carriage before. The excitement was evident on their faces as Henry called his orders to the horses.

Their driver was well trained and took them for a short, historic tour of the town. As they rode along, Tom held Samantha's hand. They listened to Henry's stories about the rich history of this little town and smiled at one another as they rode. Shortly, the carriage ride had ended and they had arrived back at the little office already. Henry tied the horses to their hitching post then proceeded to escort Tom and Samantha down from the carriage.

'Thank you Henry, for your history lesson and the ride', Tom told him as the young couple bid him 'good-bye'. Samantha told Tom how much she had enjoyed their carriage ride. 'I'm glad you liked it', Tom replied. Now, the nerves were really beginning to work on Tom as they walked arm in arm down the sidewalk. The next part of the surprise was almost upon them as they approached a park bench near a lovely fountain. Samantha sat quietly as Tom rehearsed in his mind exactly what he was about to say to her. Finally, when he felt that he was ready, Tom knelt down on one knee and took hold of Samantha's small hand. Samantha looked down into Tom's blue eyes and smiled sweetly.

'Samantha, you know that you are the love of my life and I don't know what I would do without you', Tom started. Samantha held tightly to Tom's hand as he continued. 'Would you do me the honor of being my wife?' 'I want to spend the rest of my life, with you at my side', he told her. As Tom pulled the ring out of his pocket, a tear rolled down Samantha's cheek.

Tom placed the ring on Samantha's finger and felt a lump develop in his throat as he waited for her answer. At this point, the tears were over-flowing from Samantha's eyes and she found it hard it to speak. When she finally got her bearings, Samantha answered Tom with 'Yes, I will be honored to be your wife'. Tom stood up and kissed his fiancé, taking her in his arms and holding her tight.

The two young 'lovebirds' sat and enjoyed the warm, July sunshine as they talked about their future. What a fabulous day this had been for the both of them. But the day wasn't over with yet! Tom still had a few surprises in store for Samantha but the proposal part was over. He had worried about what Samantha's answer to his surprising question was going to be. All that mattered was that she had said yes! And Tom couldn't wait to begin his new life with Samantha.

Yep, the best girl for him sat next to him now and it wouldn't be long before he would call her his wife. Lightning sounded off in a distance as Tom and Samantha walked through the park, hand in hand. 'Maybe we should head back to Swanton', Tom told Samantha. As they drove towards home, the radio station played fun, upbeat songs for a summer's day.

Samantha couldn't wait to tell her Mother the wonderful news! What a great birthday this had been so far! As long as the weather permitted, Tom had planned to take Samantha to the final summer fireworks display in Swanton. This would be the finale for their summer festivities in the little town.

As they arrived back at Tom's house, Samantha asked if she could call her Mother. Katie congratulated them then showed Samantha the telephone in the dining room. Samantha thought how odd it sounded to say that she was engaged! But, oh it was bliss! Samantha told her Mother all about her wonderful birthday with Tom. All, except the engagement part that is. She wanted to tell her Mother that part in person.

Tom and Samantha arrived at the fairgrounds where there was plenty of activity going on. The carnival rides were over-flowing with people who were looking for a spine-chilling ride on this July afternoon. Samantha loved to watch the young children play the children's games and loved it even more when they won a big prize! It reminded her of when she and her brothers went to the fair when they were young.

Tom and Samantha walked around for a while until they got hungry. Tom got them each a corn dog then they sat down to enjoy them. 'Fair food is the best' Tom told Samantha when they had finished their treat. Samantha asked if Tom would ride the Ferris wheel with her after their stomachs were settled. He was a bit apprehensive, but said that he would go with her if she insisted.

'Tom, this has been the best day ever', Samantha exclaimed to him. 'I'm glad that you have enjoyed yourself, Samantha' he replied. As they walked over to the Ferris wheel ticket line, Tom leaned over and gave his fiancé a kiss. He could barely contain his happiness that Samantha had said yes to his proposal! Eventually, it was their turn to board the ride, so they took their seats and buckled themselves in. Tom was nervous but for his love, he would do anything!

After the Ferris wheel ride, they walked over to the carnival game area. 'Do you want me to win you a prize?' Tom asked Samantha. 'Sure' she answered with a big smile. Tom gave the young man a dollar so that he could play the 'Skee ball game. Tom's first try was unsuccessful, so he handed another dollar to the young man. This time, Tom got the maximum number of points. He asked Samantha to pick her prize. She chose a big brown teddy bear with a big red bow around his neck. As Tom handed Samantha the big bear, he whispered in her ear, 'I Love You'.

Samantha giggled at her cute, cuddly bear as they walked towards the grandstand to watch the fireworks show. They found their seats before the crowd began to get much bigger. The seats filled up fast as young and old alike got comfortable and waited for the finale show. Each year, the fairgrounds folks always had two fireworks shows, one on the fourth of July and the other one towards the end of July. Both were fantastic shows! This night would be the perfect ending to a better than perfect day. A day that Tom and Samantha would not soon forget!

Needless to say, when Cindy was told the big news, she was ecstatic! 'Samantha, I am so happy for the two of you', she told Samantha. Samantha and Cindy sat on the front porch swing that evening when Samantha got home from the fireworks. 'Mom, I can't believe that he asked me to marry him'! Samantha said to her Mother. Cindy told Samantha that they would have a lot of planning to do for the 'big day'. 'I know', Samantha said.

'We'll need to make a list of everything that you'll need to do before the wedding', Cindy told her daughter. Samantha replied, 'It will be fun to help arrange all that I want for the decorations and the bouquets and whatever else that we'll need'. Cindy knew that Samantha really didn't know what was entailed in the planning of a wedding. So, she intended to teach Samantha the basics.

The next morning, Cindy and Samantha sat and talked again about the flowers and table decorations. Although the exact date was still undecided, Samantha wanted to get married the next year, possibly, in the fall. Samantha loved autumn so it was only fitting to her. There would be plenty to tend to before the wedding date but Samantha would have plenty of help.

Samantha would continue working for the rest of the summer to help with the wedding fund that she and Tom had started at the bank. The excitement was beginning to build over this new chapter in Samantha's life and she was more than ready to be a part of Tom's life for the rest of hers.

Chapter twenty

As Samantha returned to school in the fall, she realized that a year from now she would be Mrs. Tom Halson! That was a strange thought to Samantha, not only that she would be a wife but also a college student at the same time. Many thoughts were going through Samantha's mind as she studied for her algebra test that night. She no longer had Carol for a roommate so she now had to get acquainted with a new one. Her name was Tonia and she was from Illinois. She was from a family of pig farmers who had carried on the tradition for fifty years.

Tonia was embarrassed to talk about her family's way of life. Samantha assured her that there was nothing to worry about. 'We all have different means to feed our families', Samantha told her new friend. Samantha told Tonia that she too grew up on a farm and that her Dad also raised farm animals. Tonia felt better after their talk and the two talked for a while before it was time for bed.

The next few days, Samantha stayed busy with her classes. When she found an extra moment, she jotted down ideas in her notebook for her wedding. Tonia was surprised that Samantha was already engaged at her young age. She had told Samantha that her boyfriend was too shy to even think of asking her to marry him. At least not any time soon anyway!

The heart-warming feeling that Samantha got when she thought about Tom kept her going through the rigorous schedule at school. Not only had Samantha signed up for a second History class she also was volunteering at a nearby clinic. Samantha's heart melted when she saw the sweet, innocent faces of the young children that she helped care for at the clinic. She had always had a love for children, so it was only natural that she had taken a job working with them each week.

Back at home, Cindy had been working on Samantha's wedding arrangements. Samantha was happy to have her Mother help her with anything that she could, so Cindy did everything in her power to help make this wedding a fabulous and spectacular event! As long as Cindy had a 'say-so' in the matter, she intended not to leave anything to chance. This would be her daughter's special day and she would not settle for anything less than perfect for her!

Samantha had chosen periwinkle and peach as the two main colors for the wedding. Melissa had agreed to be Samantha's Maid of Honor, so this made her very happy to have her best friend stand up with her. Tom and Samantha had opted to have the meal catered in. This would give the women in the family a chance to relax and enjoy the festivities that day. Samantha wasn't having her family working to prepare food on her day! She needed them all to celebrate with her instead.

So many things were happening in Samantha's life that she sometimes felt over-whelmed by it all. Looking for a place to live was the furthest from her mind, but she knew eventually, she and Tom would need to find their own place. The days seemed like they were passing rather quickly as Tom and Samantha made plans to spend their lives together, together as a young married couple. The thought made Samantha get choked up sometimes but she knew that they would be O.K.

The two of them had been through many life-changing events in their years as friends but the future meant everything to them. Both were determined to stay focused and ready to stand up to any one thing that might challenge their strength as a couple.

As Tom and Samantha spoke with the pastor at the small Baptist Church where they would be married, fond memories flooded back to Samantha about Sunday school classes here at this very Church. Samantha hoped that she and Tom would be blessed with children that they too could take to Sunday school. As they talked with the pastor about the ceremony, Samantha held tight to Tom's hand. It would not be long before they would be saying their vows here.

After their consultation with Pastor Mike, he bid them well and told them that he would see them in Church on Sunday. In a matter of weeks, they would be husband and wife and Samantha was over-joyed! As the preparations were completed for the 'big day', everyone felt a sense of excitement for the two young folks ready to begin a new life together. 'Something Old' was one of Grandma Berta's favorite handkerchiefs. It had been given to her by her Grandmother on her wedding day and she had treasured it ever since. 'Something Blue' was a pretty little lacy garter that Samantha had picked out for herself. Everything was falling into place perfectly, Samantha thought as she put her pretty things away.

Tom was very patient as Samantha helped finalize plans for their special day. He wanted her to be happy more than anything he had wished for in his life. He had stood by his vow to stay on the straight and narrow and it was going to stay that way! Tom wanted to make Samantha happy no matter what! It was a ways away but Tom could not wait to marry Samantha and make her a happy woman!

Although they had looked at several possible places to live, Tom and Samantha were still up in the air about where they would be living after they were married. It was a given that they would need to be close to both schools so that made their decision even more difficult! Tom assured Samantha that it would be alright and asked that she keep praying that they would find a place soon. For many weeks, they continued searching until finally, they found the 'one'.

In a quiet little neighborhood, Tom and Samantha had found a cute one bedroom apartment not far from Tom's school. About a twenty minute drive was all it would be for Tom's commute and around fifteen minutes for Samantha. Now, the big chore of getting ready to move was also on their list of things 'to do' before the wedding. As Tom and his fiancé drove back to Swanton, Samantha made some mental notes of all the additional things that they would need for their apartment.

Tom had not yet told Samantha where they were going on their honeymoon, so she began to quiz Tom as he drove. 'Is it tropical?' she asked him. 'I can't say', Tom told her. 'Well, I'll need to know what to pack, sir', Samantha told him sharply. Tom assured her that he would let her know soon enough what she would need to bring on their honeymoon! Samantha's curiosity was killing her but she trusted Tom to take her someplace very special!

When they arrived back at Samantha's house, they told Cindy about the apartment they had found. Cindy told them that it sounded convenient for the two of them as they talked about the cute little place with her. Although she would miss Samantha terribly, Cindy knew that it was time to let her begin this new chapter in her life.

In just a matter of a few weeks, Tom and Samantha would be husband and wife. Cindy couldn't be happier for the two of them, but she felt an empty space in her heart, a space that Samantha had filled since the day that she was born. Cindy wished that William could be here for Samantha's big day. But in her heart, she knew that he would be there in spirit. Just the same, Scott had agreed to give Samantha away and was very proud to be there for his little sister.

Last minute details were being taken care of by Katie and Cindy as the wedding date approached. Everything seemed to be going well, actually better than expected, so the two Moms assured Samantha that all was well with the preparations. The final fitting for Samantha's dress was this afternoon at 3:00 P.M. Samantha rode with her Mother to the Bridal Salon after the two stopped for a quick lunch in town.

The beautiful white organza gown that Samantha had chosen hung inside the dressing room of the lavishly furnished Bridal Salon. The young woman led Samantha to the dressing room in the back of the shop. Samantha called to her Mother for her help in trying on the gown one last time. Cindy assisted her young daughter so she could try on the dress again. There had been some alterations done since she had last tried it on, so they hoped that it was perfect!

Cindy helped Samantha by buttoning the back of the beaded gown then she helped her out of the small dressing room into the room with the large mirrors. Samantha stepped up onto the platform in front of the mirror in order to see the beautiful dress from all sides. 'Samantha, it is perfect', Cindy told her with a tear in her eye. 'You are absolutely beautiful in it!' Cindy continued. 'Thanks, Mom', Samantha told her Mother. 'Mom, do you think that Tom will like it?' Samantha asked innocently. Cindy responded to her daughter with, 'He will absolutely love it!'

When Samantha was finished admiring the dress, Cindy helped her get it safely back inside the garment bag so they could take it home until the 'big day'! As Cindy and Samantha drove back home, Samantha asked her Mother if she had been nervous to get married to her Father. 'Yes, we were young and in love, but we were both nervous about taking a big step in our lives back then', Cindy told Samantha. 'I'm sure I'll be O.K., Mom'. 'I just need to keep a positive attitude', Samantha told her.

As she slept that evening, Samantha dreamed of warm, sandy beaches and the beautiful blue waters of the ocean, the waves rushing to the shore. A tranquil setting played out in her dreams as she sat on the warm sand and enjoyed the solitude that it brought to her soul.

When Samantha awoke the next morning, she thought about her peaceful dream. Maybe this meant that Tom would be taking her someplace beautiful like in her dream! Samantha smiled at the thought and began getting ready for the day ahead of her. Today, Tom's groomsmen were going to the tuxedo shop for their final fittings. Tom had told Samantha that he would meet her there at 11:00 A.M. this morning. After breakfast, Samantha sat and talked with her Mother for a while. They both enjoyed these special moments together for they both knew that these times would become less often once Samantha was married.

When Samantha looked at Tom in his tuxedo, she smiled at how handsome he was in it. He returned the smile and mouthed the words, 'I Love You' to Samantha, as he stood in front of the mirror at the tuxedo shop. It was so hard to contain the happiness between them but Tom and Samantha somehow managed to keep their minds to the tasks at hand. In only two weeks, they would be Mr. and Mrs. Tom Halson and nothing could come between them and their love!

Tom had prayed each night that he would be a good husband to Samantha. And he also prayed that they would remain 'in love' for the rest of their lives. The vows that they intended to make were promises to each other to remain faithful and true to one another. Tom's nerves had not been a problem until these last couple of weeks before the wedding. He hoped that they didn't show themselves to Samantha.

As to be expected, Samantha had wondered many times what it would be like to be married to Tom. A case of nerves had given Samantha an upset stomach these past few days. She hoped that her nerves would calm down before too long, especially before the wedding! The final countdown to their wedding date had begun just a couple of weeks ago. All preparations had been done and the final details finished. It had been a learning experience for Samantha because she had no idea what was needed to plan a wedding. Thanks to Cindy and Katie, the festivities were planned to a 'T'. There was nothing left to do but wait and Samantha was having a hard time with it at this point!

Cindy and Samantha were enjoying their supper one evening before the ceremony, when Samantha told her Mother of her queasy stomach, just waiting for the big day to arrive. Cindy then proceeded to tell Samantha about the day that she married William. "I was so nervous that my Mother sat with me as I got dressed that day'. Cindy continued, 'My Mother kept telling me what a nice young man that I was marrying', Cindy told Samantha. "It helped to know that my Mother approved of your Dad and wanted us to be happy', Cindy told Samantha.

The talk with her Mother helped to calm Samantha down some. She had told Cindy that she would be there for her also and she was thankful for that. At 3:00 A.M., on the morning of Samantha's wedding day, Samantha awoke with a start. She had just awoken from a dream, a dream where she had missed her wedding! As she got her bearings again, Samantha realized that it had been a dream, a real bad dream!

As she settled back down into her bed again, she thought about how awful it would be to miss your own wedding. What a nightmare that would be! She managed to fall asleep again after calming herself with a prayer. Samantha needed her rest for the long day ahead of her which would begin her new life with a wonderful new husband.

Cindy was up early, as usual, and had begun brewing a pot of coffee. Today, her 'baby' would be getting married to a great guy! She smiled to herself as she sat and enjoyed her morning coffee in the kitchen. Eventually, Samantha joined her Mother in the kitchen. 'Should I make us some scrambled eggs for breakfast?' Cindy asked Samantha. 'Sure, that would be great', Samantha answered. Samantha helped by making some toast to go with their eggs.

The two women sat and enjoyed their breakfast together. Cindy could tell that Samantha was apprehensive about her big day, so she grabbed her small hand and prayed with her after their meal. Samantha thanked her Mother and gave her a big hug before going upstairs to take a relaxing bubble bath before her big day began. The wedding was at 2:00 P.M., which gave Samantha a few hours to get her things together.

At the Church, Cindy helped the other girls get ready. Samantha was happy to have her Mother there to calm her if she needed her to. The girls were happy for their friend Samantha on this beautiful day that had been given her. In another room at the Church, Tom paced the floor. Back and forth he walked, until his best man, Garth, advised him to relax and take a deep breath. This was the most important day of Tom's life and he had every right to be nervous! He sat down for a moment and tried to calm himself down before it got the best of him.

Tom's thoughts went to his young fiancé and the many years that they had been friends. Years that had led them to this day in time! With his anxiety calmed, Tom went about getting ready. Back in Samantha's dressing room, Cindy was busy helping the girls where they needed her. She had also once again, calmed Samantha's butterflies as she helped her daughter with the lovely veil that she had chosen to wear with her dress.

Samantha's Maid of Honor, Melissa looked stunning in her dress as well as the rest of the girls in her wedding party. She had decided that they had made a beautiful choice in the color of the dresses for each of them. As they busied themselves with make-up and hairdos, there was knock on the door. It was Charles, informing his Mother that his brother's shoes were too big. The tuxedo shop would send another pair over for him so there was no need to worry, Charles had told his Mother.

There was no need to worry Samantha over a pair of shoes, so Cindy kept it to herself and went about helping again. It turned out that one of the girls needed a pair of pantyhose, so it was Cindy to the rescue! She had packed a few extra things in a bag, just in case the girls needed something and it had paid off. Cindy herself began getting dressed for the wedding after helping the others. She put on her locket that William had given her, along with the new dress that she had bought.

'Mom, you look fantastic', Samantha told her Mother. She continued with, 'Dad would be so proud to see you if he were here'! Cindy assured her daughter that her Dad would be here in spirit on her 'special day'. As the girls finished getting ready, Melissa noticed that nobody had their bouquet yet, so she hurried to Tom's dressing room. 'Tom, I need your keys', Melissa told him. 'We've forgotten the flowers in your car!' Tom gave Melissa the keys so she could take the flowers to everyone.

By the time that Melissa had given the girls their bouquets it was almost time for the ceremony. As the time drew nearer, Cindy kissed Samantha and whispered, 'I Love You' to her before going to take her seat in the Church sanctuary, with the rest of the family. Samantha took one last look in the mirror before leaving the dressing room.

Scott took his sister's arm and asked if she was ready. She answered, 'Yes I am' with a big smile on her face. Soft, classical music played over the speaker, as they made their way down the long hallway to the Church sanctuary. Friends and family awaited Samantha's arrival as the 'Wedding March' began to play. Samantha took a deep breath and held tight to her brother's arm as they began their walk down the aisle. The smiles on everyone's faces were a welcome sight as Samantha and Charles made their way slowly, down the aisle.

For a split second, Samantha's dream flashed back to her. Just to be sure that this was for real Samantha looked over at Tom to see his handsome smiling face looking back at her. She then realized that this was really happening after all! Yes, this truly was a dream, a dream-come-true for Samantha. The man of her dreams, stood before her now. Ready to make a commitment that they both would strongly abide by.

With this commitment, they would begin their lives together as husband and wife and look to each other along the way for the strength to face whatever obstacles came their way. This truly had been 'a match made in heaven' and it was about to be sanctified and witnessed by all who looked on!

THE END!!